Angels
for
Abigail

<+><+><+>

By Kitty Kaye
Cover Illustrated by Debbe Femiak

*To all the angels who have
touched my life,
whether I was aware of them
or not.*

FOREWORD

It doesn't matter if you believe in angels.
While this story does involve three angels
and the family they came to help, it is also a story
that deals with the understanding of how
the choices we make effect not just the quality and outcome
of our lives, but the lives of those around us as well.
Will we forfeit our lives to a series of poor choices,
or will we live wisely and achieve success?
Ultimately, the choice is ours.

This is more than just a story about angels.
This is a story of a family learning to make good choices,
as well as the antics they face along the way.
Laugh, love, and live along with the Carter family
as they try to figure out how to make life a successful
and safe journey for the whole family.

- Kitty Kaye -

TABLE OF CONTENTS

CHAPTER 1
POTTY TRAINING 101

Russell Carter leaned back into his easy chair and breathed a sigh of relief. Finally, he could enjoy a moment of peace and quiet. In this family of five, moments like these were rare. Chaos was more the norm for this household.

Just to reassure himself that the whole family was present and accounted for, he took a look around their single-level, ranch-style house. Joy sat curled up on her bed, diligently typing away on her laptop.

Joy! he chuckled to himself. She was their firstborn, and Joy was not her true name. Her birth name was Harmonie Lane, but she had been dubbed "Joy" in her teenage years, since her attitude was less than joyful.

Probably chatting online with someone she shouldn't be, Russ mused to himself, but he would let it go this time. He didn't want to interrupt this moment of tranquility.

Through the living room window, he could see his fifteen-year-old son, Corey, racing around the yard on his ATV, followed by his friend, Ryan. Corey was the easiest of the three children but, being a boy, he could certainly find plenty of mischief to get himself into.

Probably tearing up the front lawn, he smiled to himself, *but we'll deal with it later.*

Seven-year-old Holly was playing with some dolls on the floor of her bedroom. As hyperactive as she was, it was rare for her to stop moving long enough to play with dolls. However, the present activity was keeping her occupied, and Dad was thankful for that.

A movement in the kitchen caught Russell's eye, and he turned just in time to see his wife breeze past the doorway. Twenty years of marriage, and Abigail Carter still caused his heart to skip a beat. In his eyes, she was just as beautiful as the day they said, "I do."

Russ let out an audible sigh, and reached over to pick up the remote. It was just about time for the game to start, and it looked like he had the television all to himself for a change. He flipped to the sports channel, and seeing it was commercial time, decided to respond to the call of nature before the game started.

Russell walked nonchalantly into the bathroom, where his peaceful mood suddenly took an abrupt turn. The toilet was a hideous mess, not much different than the outhouse he had used at camp as a kid. Didn't anyone in this family know what that silver lever on the side of the tank was capable of? This was the twenty-first century, complete with functional, indoor plumbing.

Russ growled and bellowed out, "Everyone front and center!!"

It was a call that everyone dreaded - the call to family meeting. When Dad roared, it always meant a lecture was sure to follow. It was Dad's way of indicating that he was not happy about something, and they were all going to hear about it.

From her room, Joy groaned and dropped the laptop onto her bed. She was seventeen years old and didn't need to be treated like a baby, but she knew better than to ignore her father at a time like this.

From the kitchen, Mom groaned and opened the front door. She called to Corey to let him know he needed to join the meeting with the rest of his family.

Holly was the only one who came running. She was eager to please, and if Daddy had something to say, she wanted to be the first to hear it.

So, as usual, Holly was on the scene before everyone else. She was a bit surprised to see that this family meeting would take place in the bathroom. However, even at her young age, she had already learned not to question her father's judgment.

Corey entered the kitchen, took his helmet off, and asked Mom what was up. She explained that there was a family meeting in the bathroom. He knit his brows together in a puzzled look, not sure that he had heard her correctly.

"In the bathroom?" he questioned.

Mom shrugged her shoulders and replied, "Don't worry about it. Just do as your father says."

Joy was naturally the last to arrive, rolling her eyes in anticipation of what was to come. As she joined her family in the bathroom, she realized the air was less than pleasant.

"Smells like a stinkin' outhouse in here," she muttered.

"That's right!" Dad chimed out jubilantly, glad that someone had already 'caught wind' of the purpose of this meeting. "That is exactly why we are all gathered here in the bathroom like one happy family!"

No one dared to speak a word as Russell continued on his tyrant.

"Let me explain how indoor plumbing works," he continued, as he approached the polluted toilet. "This modern convenience is called a toilet. It houses a tank which sits on top of a toilet bowl. Does anyone know what's inside the tank?"

Joy groaned and rolled her eyes again. Did he really expect them to answer his foolish questions? But Holly anxiously raised her hand, being the only willing participant in this family meeting.

"I know - it has water in it. Right, Daddy?" she asked.

Dad pointed to her and said, "Right you are, sweetie!"

He glanced around at the remainder of the family and said, "What you people don't seem to understand is the importance of this little, silver lever located conveniently on the side of the tank."

Joy groaned again and said, "Oh, good, potty training 101!"

Dad ignored her comment and continued with his explanation. "When this little lever is depressed, the water from the tank flows down into the toilet bowl, circles around the basin, and flushes all your problems out the drain. Using this shiny, little lever routinely will keep the toilet bowl clean, and consequently, the air will stay fresher in here."

Joy could take no more. She spouted off, "I'm depressed, and I have had enough of this little, family meeting! Are we done yet? I have better things to do than stand around in the bathroom discussing how toilets work!"

Dad looked around and decided he had made his point. "Yeah, I guess that about covers it," he said. "Meeting adjourned."

Joy stormed off to her room. Corey quietly exited, anxious to get back to riding his ATV with his buddy. Mom breezed back into the kitchen, and resumed her position at the kitchen sink. Holly reached over, tugged on her father's sleeve, and said, "I will try my best to remember to always use the little, silver lever, Daddy."

Dad sighed out loud, both wishing all of his kids were so eager to please, and at the same time, knowing that he had just ruined his peaceful afternoon of watching the game.

"I know you will, sweetheart," he said, as he rubbed her head. "You're Daddy's little girl, aren't you?"

He bent down to give her a hug, and she reached up to gently kiss his cheek.

"Why don't you run along and play now. Daddy needs to try to fix this toilet."

She smiled sweetly and ran out of the bathroom. Russell picked up the plunger and resigned himself to one of the dirty duties that came along with being a father. With this much refuse in the toilet bowl, this would be no easy task.

In her room, Joy was raging. Did he really find it necessary to give the whole family a lesson on how to flush a toilet? Did he think they were babies? She was almost an adult now. She most certainly did not need to be reprimanded for not flushing the toilet.

She grabbed her purse and headed for the front door. As she passed through the kitchen, her mother asked where she was going. Her reply consisted of one single syllable -

"OUT!!"

Corey had raced back outside to join Ryan, who had been waiting patiently on his ATV.

"What was that all about?" his friend asked.

"Don't ask," Corey replied, putting his helmet back on. "Let's just ride."

They started their ATVs and soon began racing around the yard again. Holly, hearing the roar of their engines, decided to go watch their amateur performance. She ran across the yard, and climbed up into the apple tree where she could view the activity, but not be in the way.

Around and around they raced, tearing up lawn here, with a little gravel flying there. Holly giggled with glee, finding this way more exciting than watching television or playing with dolls.

Corey paused for a moment, and his buddy quickly came to a stop beside him. Lifting the shield of his helmet, he said, "Watch this. I've been working on this stunt for a few weeks now."

He accelerated and leaned to one side of his ATV, apparently trying to accomplish a two-wheeled performance. However, losing control of his ATV, he instead veered toward the patio furniture sitting in the yard. Realizing he needed to do something quickly, he yanked his handle bar sharply to the left, banked off the roots of the huge pine tree which stood austerely in the front yard, and careened directly into the side of his mother's brand new car.

Ryan pulled up beside Corey and shut off his ATV. Whipping off his helmet, he said, "Ah, man, right into your mom's brand new car! You're as good as dead!"

Inside the house, Mom had heard the crash, too.

"Russell," she called, "please tell me that noise was you working in the bathroom."

Dad, still struggling to unclog the toilet, had not heard the crash. "What noise?" he called back.

Mom didn't want to know the source of the noise, but knew it needed to be investigated.

"I think we need to check it out," she called back.

Together they exited the house, and Abigail's jaw dropped in horror when she spotted the massive dent in the side of her car. Her mouth opened and closed a few times, but no words came out.

It was not so with Russell. He roared, "What were you thinking, Corey? Or were you thinking at all? Didn't you see your mother's car sitting in the driveway? How could you have missed it?"

Corey looked at the dent, then back at his father before he innocently replied, "I didn't miss it, Dad."

In the wake of Corey's crash, no one realized that Holly had stood up on her perch in the apple tree. As she leaned forward to get a better view of the events, she lost her balance and tumbled to the ground.

Her screams of agony quickly disrupted the trauma of Corey's crash. Everyone rushed to her side, where it immediately became apparent that she had broken her arm.

"We need to get her to the hospital," Abigail exclaimed.

"We'll have to take my truck since it's obvious that your car is currently out of commission," Russell added.

Corey quickly volunteered to stay home and keep an eye on things. He had already caused enough commotion, and the best thing for him at the moment was to stay home and keep out of the way.

"Does anyone know where Joy is?" Dad asked.

"Joy?" Mom repeated.

Joy had left in a huff with no explanation as to where she was headed, or when she would be returning. At this very moment, she was, in fact, at a wild party at her friend, Amber's house. Although no one there was of a legal age, they had somehow managed to acquire a couple of six-packs of beer, and they were wasting no time at all in disposing of them. She had no idea of the dilemmas piling up at home, nor did she even care. In her teenage frame of mind, life was all about her, and no one else in her family really mattered.

<+><+><+>

CHAPTER 2
A CRY FOR HELP

Abigail Carter sat quietly in the empty Franklin County Congregational Church. The solitude of her surroundings was a sharp contrast to the battle that raged within her. She was glad that the church had been unlocked, but wasn't quite sure what to do now that she was here. For a moment, she felt an element of panic, and had to fight off the urge to flee. She had never been one to run from her problems, though. She knew that running had never proven to be a solution. She needed help, and this seemed like a good place to begin her search.

She glanced around at the vacant pews and found the serenity almost painful. Chaos and noise had become her way of life. She had not known that kids could cause such an extreme level of stress. Oh, she loved her children with all of her heart, naturally, but love was not the issue. More to the point was the fact that her household seemed to be out of control, and she was desperate for some type of assistance. As mother of the family, it was her task to keep order in the household, but the Carter family had become somewhat dysfunctional in recent days.

It was necessary for her to be here, she told herself. Joy and Corey were at school, and Holly was resting comfortably with her father at home, so there was no reason to rush off. She had time to sort things out, find a little guidance, and try to bask in a few moments of seclusion and solitude. The trauma of yesterday's events had pushed her beyond her human limit. She had known as soon as she climbed out of bed this morning that she had to find a way to calm the storm that brewed within her.

In the world outside the church, it was a beautiful day. It was late August, and still comfortably warm. Today sported a clear, blue sky with ample sunshine, but even the sun had not been able to break through the cloudy mood inside of her. With nerves that were frayed, she felt like she could explode at any minute. Crying would probably help dissipate this mood, but if she started, would she be able to stop? Just the thought of tears made her eyes water and, before she knew it, the dam had burst and the tears began to flow.

She cried for her children. She cried for her family. She cried for herself. She cried for the frustration of not understanding what she could do to help her children, and not knowing how to bring order back into her chaotic household.

Joy seemed to have gone wild and was completely out of control. Abigail could not understand what had happened to Joy. As a child, she had been such a sweet, happy, little girl. Yet, now she wouldn't listen to a word of advice that either of her parents tried to offer. She wanted to be free and independent, but she was headed down the wrong road. Abigail suspected she was pursuing bad habits, but didn't really want to know if she was. It would break her heart to know, she reasoned within herself. Yet on the other hand, she should know so she could help her. The argument in her mind spun around and around.

To get away from the confusion of Joy, she turned her thoughts to Corey. He was basically a good kid, but that dent in her car... Just the thought of it brought on another flow of tears. This had been Abigail's first new car. They had scraped and saved for months, struggling to come up with enough money to invest in the car, and now it had a major dent in its side. How could he be so reckless? How could he have not seen the car sitting in the yard? Was he blind? Or maybe he just rides too fast. Why couldn't he slow down and think things through? Plus, if he couldn't handle an ATV, how could she know if he would be safe when it comes time to drive a car?

And Holly - oh, she was as cute as a button, and sweet as could be. However, Abigail couldn't turn her back on her for a moment. She was everywhere and into everything. Abigail hadn't cleaned up one mess, and Holly was already making another. It was like she was a perpetual toddler. How could a child move so quickly and be so mischievous? Then there was the incessant talking that could drive anyone crazy!

Abby blew her nose and dried her eyes. She needed help. She knew Russell did all he could to lend a hand, but sometimes it just wasn't enough. She needed more, so she was going to the highest power she could think of.

"God," she whispered, hardly able to speak, "My name is Abigail Carter. I know I don't come here as often as I should. Maybe that's why I'm in this situation."

She paused for a moment, reviewing the events of the last day in her mind, for what seemed the thousandth time. Then she quickly continued on, afraid the flood gate would open again, and release an unstoppable flow of tears.

"Lord, you have given me three beautiful children. I will not deny that, but I need guidance in raising them. I have tried to instill good morals and values in them, but I'm not sure I've done enough. Joy is hanging out with the wrong crowd. I'm so afraid she'll get herself into trouble.

"Corey is an impulsive boy. Now that he is driving motored vehicles, he is actually dangerous. I'm extremely worried about his safety, for one thing, but also for the property damage he causes.

"And Holly, as cute as she is, completely wears me out with her hyperactivity. I just can't stay one step ahead of her. God, if you are listening to me, I'm just asking for some help. I can't do this on my own anymore. Can you help me.....please?"

As Abigail sat quietly on the rigid, wooden church pew, she began to question herself. "God, is it me?" she asked. "Am I even qualified to be a mother? Do other parents have the same type of issues I am having? Sometimes, I just feel totally inadequate as a mother, like I just don't have what it takes to meet the needs of my children."

She hung her head, and cradled her face in her hands. Maybe this was some kind of a test, a means of judging her performance and ability to endure hardships. But if it was, did she have what it took to pass the test? Would her score be less than pleasing to her, or to her family?

Abby rubbed her forehead intensely, as if trying to massage her tired brain. She paused for a moment, like she was listening for an answer to any of her questions. Then she said, "If you are there, God, would you please just give me a sign so I will know you have heard my plea? I'm not asking for a miracle, just a little guidance for my children, so they will be safe and won't make any serious mistakes that could alter the course of their lives."

Abigail sat quietly in the church for a moment, waiting for a sign from Heaven. The tinkling of tiny bells, a flash of light, or anything that could prove to her that God had heard her cry for help would be appreciated. Yet nothing happened - no lightning, no thunder, not even a gentle breeze blowing through the open window. After a few moments of complete silence, Abigail thought she could hear the chiming of a distant church bell, but she couldn't be sure that it had anything to do with her heartfelt request.

Finally, Abigail blew her nose one last time, and wiped away any sign of tears. Feeling both dejected and somehow relieved at the same time, she slowly stood and made her way back out into the afternoon sunlight.

Stepping out onto the stone steps in front of the church, Abigail took a deep breath. She was resilient, she told herself. Things might be rough right now, but she knew deep down inside that they would make it through. Maybe God hadn't given her a sign, but she knew He must have heard her. Didn't He? Wasn't there some way He could help lighten her load and give her strength during these difficult days? Was He really concerned that she, Abigail Carter, was seeking help from the very throne room of God?

CHAPTER 3
THE ASSIGNMENT

The trumpets blared, and a fervent flutter of wings filled the air. It was the call to daily meeting, and no angel dared to keep God waiting. They flew, walked, or ran as fast as they could to the majestic meeting room. Not only did they not want to keep God waiting, but each angel individually hoped that maybe this would be the day that God would choose them for an assignment.

Only the most dependable were chosen for earthly assignments. These were the angels who had earned their place in the kingdom of Heaven. They had passed all the tests, and had proven that they were worthy of any mission set before them.

When the fluttering of wings had settled and all halos were present, God, in all his glory and splendor, entered the overflowing room and took his seat at the throne of glory. A holy hush fell over the room. No matter how many times God made an appearance, it was still a breathtakingly, awesome sight.

Daniel, Gabriel, and Robert sat huddled together, waiting for the meeting to begin. They had not known each other during their earthly lifetimes, but had become an inseparable angelic trio in Heaven. Perhaps it was their sudden and untimely passing that gave them such unity in Heaven. They had each died much too young, and very unexpectedly.

Daniel had passed one snowy night as the result of a car accident. He had been caught in a blizzard while simply trying to make his way home from work. Gabriel's passing had been the result of a plane crash, traveling home on a company-owned, twin engine jet while returning from a business conference. Robby's passing happened during the heat of the summer and was mostly his own doing.

He had been out boating with friends one warm, summer afternoon. While showing off, he dove out of the boat into shallow water and failed to return to the surface. Being the joker that he was, his friends thought his failure to return to the surface was just another one of his practical jokes. By the time his friends realized something was wrong, it was too late to save him.

Now that they had found each other in Heaven, it was a rare moment that they were ever apart. Theirs was a friendship that would last throughout all of eternity, and possibly their deep desire to return to Earth was due in part to their short life spans. All three carried the feeling of not having completed their full missions while alive on Earth.

Once all angels were present and seated, God stood to address the assembly. Wings quivered in anticipation, wondering what assignments would be available today. The first options were boring and mundane - a shelter in need of a nightly patrol angel, and a call to rescue a dog stuck in a storm drain. However, when God approached the topic of the Carter family, the three angels perked up.

"Now this one just came in this morning," God said, "A distraught mother came to me seeking help for her wayward children.

"It seems the oldest child, Joy, is a teenager who is displaying quite a defiant attitude these days. She's following the wrong crowd and making some significantly poor choices. Those choices include wild parties involving alcoholic beverages and also smoking. Now we all know those are choices Heaven frowns upon, don't we angels?"

God paused to look at His host of heavenly beings, and then He continued. "These are habits Abigail is not fully aware of, and I would like to keep it that way. It would break her heart to know her child is pursuing these potentially hazardous decisions."

As God glanced around the angelic crowd, Daniel grew restless with anticipation. In his lifetime, he had been a drug and alcohol counselor. Some of his career had involved working with defiant, rebellious teenagers. He could handle Joy. He had no doubt about it.

God continued with his overview of the Carter family. "Joy has a younger brother named Corey. He is a good-hearted boy, but a little on the reckless side. He has recently caused some serious property damage, and Mom is concerned for his safety. It seems he recently created quite a stir by driving his all terrain vehicle into the side of his mother's new car. He didn't get hurt in the crash, but mom is worried the next time he won't be so lucky. It will take a busy set of wings to keep up with this young man."

Daniel looked at Gabriel, who nodded in silent agreement. Gabriel had raised two boys of his own. They had not necessarily been a family that spent a lot of time outside. Their experiences with nature had not gone much beyond an occasional picnic in the park, as Gabriel's career had followed a different path. He had been a successful stock broker who was more accustomed to wearing a suit and tie than a pair of jeans, but he knew boys. They could find mischief at every corner. He felt quite confident that he could handle Corey.

"And the youngest child is Holly," God continued. "She is a bright and happy child. However, Mom is quite worn out with trying to keep up with her. She recently took a tumble out of the family apple tree and found herself with a broken arm. She manages to continuously stay one step ahead of her parents, and leaves them both exhausted at the end of the day."

Daniel and Gabriel both turned to look at Robert, who responded with a shrug of his shoulders. He had never had children before. He was just a fun-loving guy who had bounced from one job to another and just barely made it into Heaven by the skin of his teeth, but he was game. He could handle Holly. She couldn't be any worse than his hyperactive nephew, and he had Daniel and Gabriel to back him up. He gave Daniel the "thumbs up," indicating that he was agreeable with the assignment.

God turned to his army of angelic beings and said, "This sounds like a very busy trio of children. Are there any angels who feel capable of handling the challenges they present?"

Daniel turned to Gabriel and Robert, just to make sure there were no second thoughts. Both angels responded with a nod. This seemed to be too perfect an assignment to let it slip away. This trio of angelic ambassadors was meant to tackle this trio of trouble.

So, Daniel quickly stood and bowed in obedience to the maker of the universe. When God acknowledged him, he spoke up and said, "Father, I believe Gabriel, Robert, and I would be the perfect angels for this mission."

He paused for a moment, then God said, "Continue, Daniel, explain your reasoning."

So Daniel explained his position. He had experience with drug and alcohol rehabilitation, Gabriel had raised two boys of his own, and Robert had lots of energy and could easily keep up with Holly.

God stroked his snow-white beard while listening to Daniel's appeal. It was His responsibility to find angels qualified for each mission. To send an angel who was not prepared could mean disaster to the family in need.

"Hmm," God said, still stroking his beard, "but Robert has never had any children. Do you really think he can keep up with Holly?"

Daniel glanced at Robby, who only raised his eyebrows and shrugged a shoulder in response. Yet, Daniel stood his ground.

"Yes, Father," he replied, "I believe he can. Plus, Gabriel and I will be right there to help him if he needs assistance."

When God hesitated, he added, "Please, Father God, we would really like to help this family."

God paused to consider the match between the two trios. He knew that Joy would be the most challenging of the children, and He wanted to make sure this was a mission that would not fail. If His angels failed to perfect this mission, Joy would become a lost soul with a life of addiction and struggling ahead of her. He had to make sure He chose the right angel for the job.

"Abigail is naturally concerned about the safety and well-being of all her children," He explained to his congregation, "but Joy is a little more personal. At this time in her life, Joy is breaking her mother's heart. Abigail misses the little girl who used to be so happy and such an active part of her family. She is extremely concerned that Joy will get caught up in some bad habits that will take control of her life."

The three angels stopped to consider the severity of the mission. It would be their united task to keep all three children safe, and at the same time, try to keep Joy from ruining her life.

God turned and made direct eye contact with Daniel. "You were an alcohol and drug counselor in your lifetime, Daniel," He said. "I believe that you are capable of this assignment. Do you feel you could manage Joy and help her find her way back onto a positive track in life?"

Daniel eagerly nodded his head in the affirmative. If there was one thing he knew, it was the effects of drugs and alcohol on a human life. He would do all he could to rescue Joy and point her in the right direction.

"Yes, I do, Father," he replied. "I feel I could be very beneficial to Joy and the Carter family."

God smiled at the eagerness of this angelic being, and slowly nodded His head. "Okay, than it is settled. You will become Joy's guardian angel, and together with Gabriel and Robert, you will work with the Carter family. But just to be sure nothing goes awry during your time on earth, I am giving you and your partners each a silver bell to wear. If one angel is in need of assistance, he needs only to ring his bell to summon the other angels. You will need to work together as a team to see this mission through to success. And you are to remain anonymous on this assignment. The Carters are not to see you or be aware of your presence unless you feel it is a dire situation where your presence should be made known."

Daniel and Gabriel grinned from ear-to-ear, and Robby let out a less than angelic whoop. Their first real assignment! To say they were excited would have been the understatement of all time. They were nothing short of ecstatic. They would solve the problems of the Carter family and make their world a better place in which to live.

The angels were so excited to have been accepted for this assignment that they kept high-fiving each other and patting each other on the back. Finally, God spoke up.

"Boys, you have a family awaiting your help. Don't you think you should get on with your assignment?"

"Yes, God," they said unanimously, and the three angels stood to leave the assembly. As they reached the door to exit the majestic meeting room, God called out to them again.

"One final reminder before you head on your way. No unruly or wild play during your days on Earth." Turning to look directly at Robert, he added, "This is serious business, Robert. You are on a mission to help the Carter family, not on an extension of your lifetime."

Robert winced. He knew no one could hide anything from God, and God was very aware of the kind of life Robert had lived. However, those days were gone, and he would keep that in mind during his days back on Earth.

"What you do on Earth will directly affect the quality of the lives you are trying to save," God continued. "Plus, you most certainly wouldn't want to lose your wings and halo now, would you?" God paused, gave Robert a smile, knowing he would do his best for the Carters, then finished with, "And one more thing. Remember that your goal is safety for the children. Property damage takes second place."

God smiled and winked at them, then waved His hand to send them on their way. Their perfect assignment on Earth was about to begin.

CHAPTER 4
THE BIRTHDAY PARTY

The return to Earth was as quick and mysterious as their passing had been. One moment the angels were in the portals of Heaven, and the next moment they were standing on the front lawn of the Carter homestead. With all parties heading for the car, it appeared they were getting ready to depart on a family outing.

"Looks like we get to start our assignment by going to a party," said Robert, noticing the gifts being loaded into the trunk of the car.

Daniel, being the born leader, knew they had to make some quick decisions, as it appeared their mission was already in motion.

"Okay, so we are all aware of our roles, right?" he asked. "I believe I would be the most effective working with Joy, based on my history and experience."

He glanced at the other two angels, who only nodded in agreement.

"And we all agree that Gabriel would be best for Corey, correct? He has had the most experience with boys."

The other two angels once again nodded in agreement.

"So that leaves Holly for you, Robert. Do you think you can handle her?" Daniel questioned, looking from Robert to Holly.

Robby followed his gaze, looking over at Holly, who was all dressed up for the party in a frilly, little dress with ribbons in her hair. *How difficult could it be to keep up with a cute little girl like that,* he thought to himself.

"Hey, I'm in," he said. "Holly's my girl!"

The family car started to back up and as it turned, the massive dent in the side of it became quite visible. Gabe couldn't help but wince. *I guess Corey did hit it hard,* he thought to himself. *Maybe this is going to be more of an assignment than I thought.*

Suddenly, the angels realized the family car was headed right toward them. The approach was faster than they had anticipated and didn't leave them time to react. Daniel and Gabe gasped, and Robby let out a yelp. However, the car just drove right through them as if they weren't even there.

"Wow!" said Robby with a start, "for a minute I forgot we were angels."

The three angels all smiled, then jumped into action and quickly flew after the departing car. They soon caught up and slid through the roof, situating themselves as best as they could among the passengers in the car. The Carter family headed down the road, totally unaware of the three extra passengers they carried with them. They were headed to visit Abigail's sister, Carrie, for a family gathering. Her daughter, Hannah, was celebrating her sixteenth birthday and had invited the entire family to join them.

It had been difficult, as usual, to convince Joy to come along. The drawing force that finally persuaded her was that Aunt Carrie had a swimming pool in her backyard, and Joy loved to swim.

The angels were a little rumpled by the time they arrived at the party, but anxious to get to work. They flew out of the car, wondering how exactly to begin their mission. The family jumped out of the car as well, and each angel decided to simply follow their protégé along.

Joy wasted no time in heading for the pool.

"Hello, Joy," Aunt Carrie called from the patio. "I'm glad you decided to join us today."

"Nice to see you, Aunt Carrie," Joy politely called over her shoulder. "Mind if I just jump into the pool?"

"Be my guest," Carrie replied. "I'll let the kids know you're here."

Aunt Carrie watched as Joy walked intently toward the pool and gracefully slid in. She shook her head and turned to face her sister.

"It's hard to believe she is in her final year of high school," she commented. "It seems like she just started Kindergarten a few years ago."

"In some ways it seems like the years have flown by," Abigail agreed. "But with her attitude lately, I am actually looking forward to her graduating and heading to college."

"That's what the teenage attitude was designed for, Abby," Carrie stated. "To help parents let go of their children. If they were always well behaved, we would never want them to leave home!"

Abigail smiled and nodded her head in agreement. It sounded like it made sense to her.

Joy and Corey were soon joined at the pool by Carrie's children, Hannah and Kevin. The rest of the Carter family was ushered inside by Carrie and her husband, Ted, who were anxious to show off their new home improvements. Robby tagged along behind them, while Gabe and Daniel joined the teenagers out in the pool area.

Aunt Carrie was a wonderful person, but she did like to brag about her earthly possessions. She was quite pleased to point out all the fine features of their remodeling project. So involved was she in her boastful ranting, that she failed to notice the eye contact between Russell and Abigail. Abby's eyes displayed a look of pure jealousy, while Russell's showed annoyance. Not only was he irritated with Carrie's ceaseless boasting, but he also knew that now Abigail would be nagging him to remodel their family ranch.

When Carrie was finally satisfied that she had successfully presented every feature of their endeavors, she decided to show them the newest member of the family, a blue cockatiel named Jewel.

"Isn't she a beauty?" Carrie asked. "She was an early birthday present for Hannah. She has wanted a bird ever since she was little. Finally, we broke down and bought her one. She doesn't do much, just sits in her cage looking pretty, and squawks every once in awhile. But at least she's not making a mess of the house, like some of the other pets we have owned."

Carrie paused, then said, "Well, shall we set up outside? To stay inside on a gorgeous day like this would be an absolute sin."

She picked up the cake and headed for the door. Abigail, Russell, and Ted naturally followed behind, picking up what was left on the table and following Carrie out the door.

After the adults had departed, Robby stopped to take a closer look at Jewel. As he bent down to look into the cage, Jewel let out with a loud squawk. The noise scared poor Robby, who would have jumped out of his skin, if he had some.

Holly was just about to follow the adults out the door when

Jewel's squawk caught her attention. She abruptly turned around and came back to talk to her.

"What's the matter, Jewel?" she asked. She soon summed up the problem in her little, seven-year-old brain, deciding Jewel wanted companionship.

"I bet you don't want to be in the house all by yourself, do you?" she asked. "Would you like to join the rest of the family for the party? I'm sure Aunt Carrie wouldn't mind."

Holly had a true love for all animals. Her favorite place in the world was at the pet store. At this very moment, she was remembering how the clerk at the pet store carried birds just like this one around on her shoulder. Holly decided Jewel could ride on her shoulder, too.

She opened the cage and reached in to pick the bird up, but Jewel naturally resorted to the furthest corner of the cage. Holly wasn't going to give up that easily, though.

"Come on, Jewel," she insisted. "Come out and sit on my shoulder."

She continued to chase the cockatiel around the cage until Jewel became so flustered, she bolted for the open door of her cage as a means of escape. Flying past Holly, she flew to the highest perch she could find, landing on a corner of Aunt Carrie's tall, mahogany china cabinet. Glancing at Holly, she squawked and stretched out her wings before settling down. She clearly felt quite safe, roosting high above the probing hands that sought to reach her.

Holly looked up at Jewel, and a sense of panic welled up inside of her. If Aunt Carrie came back in and didn't find Jewel in her cage, Holly would be in a lot of trouble. She had to catch Jewel quickly and return her to her cage. At first, she tried jumping, but came nowhere close to reaching the top of the cabinet. Frantically, she looked around the room for a solution.

If only I had a net, Holly thought to herself. She ran to the kitchen closet, and opened the door to see if maybe Uncle Ted had a fishing net, but all the closet contained was a collection of mops and brooms. Grabbing a broom, Holly ran back and began to poke at Jewel, but the poking only caused Jewel to back up so far that

Holly could no longer see her.

With Jewel out of sight, Holly became frenzied and decided she had no other choice than to climb up the cabinet. She dropped the broom on the floor and crawled onto the bottom shelf of the cabinet, where she proceeded to climb from shelf to shelf. Just as she reached the top and made eye contact with Jewel, she lost her balance and fell backward, bringing the entire cabinet with her.

Robby had stood quietly in the corner, observing the whole situation, but not quite sure how to intervene. When the china cabinet began to tip, Robby leaped into action. If he didn't do something promptly, it would land directly on top of Holly, and it was his mission to protect this child.

As Holly started to fall, she let out a loud scream. Robby flew quickly to her aid, and an amazing thing happened. He instinctively reached out to catch the cabinet, and instead of it sailing through his unembodied hands as the car had passed through the angels at the Carter homestead, he managed to stop it just before it landed on her.

Holly fell to the floor with a thump, with dishes falling all around her, but was fortunate to have injured nothing more than her pride. She lay stunned on the floor, not quite sure what had just happened, while Robby still held the cabinet teetering above her head. He glanced around, and seeing a dining room chair close by, he dragged it over with his foot to rest the fallen cabinet on it.

The crash, along with Holly's scream, brought all parents running. They gasped when they came through the door and saw Holly curled up in a ball underneath the horizontal china cabinet.

"Holly!" Abigail screeched, as she ran to see if she was hurt.

Carrie gasped and put her hand over her mouth. Not only were her specialty plates all shattered in pieces across the floor, but Holly could have been seriously injured had the cabinet landed on her. She rushed to Abby's side to help inspect Holly.

After checking Holly over and hearing her summary of what had happened, Abigail took a look around.

"Oh, Carrie, your china!" she exclaimed. "I'm so sorry."

Carrie looked around and sighed. "Well, the bottom line is that china can be replaced. However, Holly cannot. Thank goodness that chair was there to stop the cabinet from falling any further. If it hadn't been there, who knows what might have happened."

Abigail turned to Holly and said, "Do you realize what a mess you have made, young lady? Your poor decision has cost Aunt Carrie a lot of money. What do you have to say for yourself?"

Holly hung her head and quietly whispered, "I'm sorry, Aunt Carrie. I'll clean it up for you."

"That's okay, sweetie," Aunt Carrie said. "You did make quite a mess, but I know you didn't mean any harm. Why don't you go out and play on the swing set while your mom and I clean this up. Some of these pieces are sharp, and I don't want you to cut yourself."

Holly looked at her mother, who nodded in agreement. Perhaps she was afraid she would still be reprimanded, or maybe she was excited to get off so easily, but either way, Holly didn't hesitate. She quickly ran outside to play, leaving the adults to clean up her mess.

Russ and Ted worked to upright the cabinet, while Abigail used the broom Holly had left behind to sweep up the broken pieces, and Carrie went to retrieve a dust pan. Robby could see that the parents had everything under control, so he followed along behind Holly, wondering what she could possibly get into next. And Jewel, who had watched the whole episode unfold from a perch on top of the curtain rod across the room, decided she would be safer in the shelter of her cage. So while the parents worked to restore order to the dining room, Jewel quietly retreated to the comfort of her cage.

Once outside, Holly, for a change, did as she had been instructed and headed directly for the swing set. Robby paused to survey the situation and adjust to the brightness of the sunlight. He was still contemplating how he had managed to stop the falling cabinet. Why had it not passed through his transparent hands as the car had passed through their bodies?

The teenagers seemed to be quite involved in a game of water volleyball and looked like they were enjoying themselves immensely. The sound of laughter and water splashing, along with the beauty of a bright, sunshiny day filled Robby with joy. He closed his eyes and drew in the sound of life around him while he thought about what had just happened. It seemed he had a bodily form of some type, yet somehow it was lacking in many human characteristics. Deciding to discuss this with Daniel and Gabriel, he looked around to find his cohorts.

When he spotted them lounging on the lawn chairs, he immediately burst into laughter. If they didn't look like a couple of beach bums, sprawled out on the lawn chairs wearing nothing more than sunglasses and swimsuits, then he would eat his halo. Robby glanced over toward Holly and, seeing that everything appeared to be under control, he dropped down into a lounge chair, joining his sunbathing buddies.

"You guys have the right idea," he said, stripping off his shirt. "Hey, who brought the sunblock?" he joked. "We don't want our angelic white skin to turn red! When it's time to go home, we want to go up, not down!"

"We better put this umbrella up," Gabe agreed jokingly, reaching over and pretending to put up the umbrella on the table beside him. "If we go home with a nice tan, everyone will think our mission was more like a vacation than work."

"Well, it hasn't been extremely difficult yet," Dan interjected. "In fact, I think it has been quite pleasant so far."

"Speak for yourself," Robby said. "I have already had to rescue Holly from a precarious situation."

Robby started to explain what had taken place inside, finishing with his surprise that he was able to stop the cabinet from falling. Since none of them had been on a mission before, this was all new to them. They discussed how the car had passed through them, yet Robby had managed to not only stop the cabinet from falling, but also move a chair with his foot.

"So maybe when we are doing a good deed, our bodies become personified in some way," Daniel contemplated.

"Yet still invisible?" Gabe questioned.

"I'm pretty sure we are invisible to the human eye," Daniel commented.

"I could clearly see you lounging out here beside the pool," Robert argued.

"Yes, because you are one of us," Daniel suggested. "I think we are able to see one another, but only become visible to the human eye when we deem it necessary."

"Okay, that makes sense," Robby nodded in agreement.

"Sounds logical to me," Gabriel agreed.

Just at that moment, one of the teenagers pointed in the direction of the sunbathing angels and yelled, "What's that?"

Everyone turned to see Hannah pointing toward the forest, and the angels all ducked, thinking maybe they weren't so invisible after all. All of the party participants turned toward the direction in which Hannah was pointing and, fortunately, looked right past the three angels. They all seemed to be wearing curious expressions, but then either returned a blank look toward Hannah or simply resumed their interrupted activity.

"What are you talking about?" Corey asked.

"I guess I'm just spooked," Hannah explained. "Our neighbors reported seeing a bear in the area recently. I thought I just saw him at the edge of the woods."

Robby quickly turned to see if Holly was still within eyesight. Fortunately, she had continued to play contentedly on the swing set, pushing an imaginary friend, apparently unaware of the teenager's apprehension.

"A bear, huh?" asked Daniel. "Have you guys ever seen a real, live bear?"

"No, I spent most of my life in the city," Gabe said. "I never had the good fortune of seeing a real bear."

"Oh, I've seen one," Robby was quick to interject.

"Is that right?" both angels chorused together.

"Yeah, I sure did," he grinned from ear to ear, "when I was just a little boy."

Both angels looked expectantly at him. For a moment he just continued to grin, but then finally added, "Yup, when my mom and dad took me to the zoo!"

Both angels groaned and Gabe said, "I thought you meant a wild one."

"He looked pretty wild to me," Robby laughed.

Robby then decided it was time to settle back and relax for

a few minutes. He stretched his arms out, and was ready to tuck them under his head, when he made a startling discovery.

"Hey guys, look!" he exclaimed.

The other angels casually glanced over, expecting him to point out an imaginary bear. Failing to see anything, Gabe asked "What is it, a bear?"

"No, look at this," he said, waving his arms around in the air. Both angels looked at him as if he had gone insane, not grasping the point that he was trying to make. Finally Daniel said, "I give up Robert. What are we supposed to be looking at?"

"No shadow," he said, pointing down toward the patio surface. "We don't make a shadow!"

Realizing he was right, all three of the angels stood up, waved their arms around in the air, and then began jumping up and down. Staring at the ground, they all tried to find some sign of a shadow.

It would have been comical, had anyone been able to see them. They resembled a flock of turkeys, flapping their wings and strutting around. So preoccupied were they with this phenomena that they failed to notice Holly had lost interest in the swing set and had moved on to other interests.

The parents had finally finished their cleaning duty inside the house and were just returning to the task of setting up the picnic table for the party when Abigail asked, "Where's Holly?"

The angels immediately stopped strutting and looked around. Holly had vanished. She was simply nowhere to be seen.

"Ah, man," said Robby, "how did she disappear so fast?"

"Do you want us to come with you?" Daniel asked, as Robby prepared to go find her.

"No, she can't be too far away," Robby replied. "She was just there a minute ago. I should be able to find her quickly. You need to stay and monitor the pool."

"Remember the bells," Gabe called over his shoulder to Robert, who was already on his way to find Holly. "We'll take a look around the yard. Just give us a ring if you need anything."

The parents also split up and began searching the area. Robert flew ahead of them to see what he could find. Holly didn't seem to be in the backyard, so he decided to venture into the forest.

It didn't take long before he spotted her. It appeared she was chasing a butterfly, which was leading her deeper into the woods. Robby needed to find a way to turn her around. He decided to try to blow the little butterfly back toward the house and direct Holly out of the forest.

Robby got himself into position and gently began to blow on the butterfly. Just when he thought his plan was working, he heard a branch snap behind him and turned to find himself face-to-face with the biggest, meanest-looking black bear he had ever seen. He had no idea they grew this big.

He knew he had to think fast. It was his responsibility to protect Holly and this bear was way too close. Somehow, he needed to get her to head back toward the house and, hopefully, turn the bear around in the opposite direction.

He took a fleeting look at Holly while his mind raced, and gasped when he realized she had spotted the bear as well.

"A bear," she whispered in awe.

Unfortunately, she didn't seem to be afraid of the bear, as Robby had hoped she would be. Instead, she seemed to be fascinated with it. In fact, it looked like she was heading his way.

Robby knew he had to do something fast to create a distance between beast and child. He quickly grabbed a stick and threw it in the opposite direction from where Holly stood, hoping to distract the bear. He breathed a sigh of relief when he saw the bear turn toward the direction in which he had thrown the stick. With all his might, he blew on the butterfly and sent him fumbling through the air.

Fortunately, it was the distraction he was looking for. Holly seemed to completely lose interest in the bear as her butterfly tumbled through the air.

"Where are you going, little butterfly?" she asked, chasing after it.

Unfortunately for Robby, her movement caught the attention of the bear, which suddenly turned around and headed in her direction.

Looking over his shoulder to assure that Holly was safely

heading toward the house, Robby rushed toward the bear in an attempt to keep him distracted. He rustled branches and threw sticks, quickly gaining the bear's full attention. However, now that he had done so, he didn't have a clue what to do next. He began to run further into the woods, and the bear followed close behind him.

I wonder if he can see me, Robby thought to himself.

Forgetting he was an angel, Robby did what would have come natural to any human brain. In his desperation to get away from the bear, he decided to climb a tree. To his misfortune, the bear stopped at the foot of the very tree he had ascended. Panicking, Robby decided it was time to call in some reinforcement. He rang his bell to summon Daniel and Gabriel for some assistance.

Both angels had watched Holly emerge from the forest and wondered what had become of Robert. When their bells rang, they quickly flew into action.

It didn't take long for them to locate Robby, teetering at the top of a tree with the bear firmly planted at the base. They worked together, rustling branches to direct the bear onto a path that led him away from Robby's tree and further into the woods. They breathed a sign of relief when he finally disappeared into the darkness of the forest.

Returning to Robby, they watched as he descended from his perch at the top of the tree.

"Thanks for the rescue, guys," Robby said, as he brushed himself off.

The other two angels only chuckled.

"What did you think he was going to do?" Gabe asked. "Kill you? You're already dead!"

Robby paused to think about it for a moment, and then he quickly replied, "It's only human nature to be a little scared when a bear is chasing you."

Daniel smiled and said, "But that's what we're trying to tell you, Robby. You're not human anymore! You didn't have to climb a tree. You could have just flown away."

"Oh, yeah," Robby said, "I keep forgetting that. Being an angel on Earth is different than being an angel in Heaven. Up there, it's easy to remember you can fly."

"I'm sure we will have time to get used to it," Gabriel suggested. "Who knows how long we will be hanging out with the Carter family."

"My mission will definitely be shorter than yours since Joy is the oldest child," Daniel confessed, "but right now I think we better get back to those we were sent to protect."

The angels returned to the family gathering, and fortunately, the rest of the party proceeded without incident. Finally, with the festivity drawing to a close, the Carter family decided it was time to head home.

"Can I have a balloon, Aunt Carrie?" Holly asked before leaving.

"Well, you most certainly can," Carrie replied. "Let's just tie it around your cast so you won't lose it."

Aunt Carrie tied the balloon to Holly's cast, and Holly grinned from ear-to-ear.

"Oh, and before you leave, I have something else for you," Aunt Carrie remembered.

She ran into the house and came out with a coin in her hand.

"When your mom called and told me you had broken your arm, I got you a new shiny dollar coin to add to your collection," she explained.

Holly giggled and gave her aunt a big hug.

"Thank you, Aunt Carrie. I'll put it away as soon as I get home so it doesn't get lost," she grinned.

Holly gave her aunt one last hug and followed the rest of the family down the driveway. They stopped beside the car while mom and dad said their final farewells. As the adults talked, Holly investigated her new coin. Suddenly, it fell out of her grasp and began to roll out toward the road.

Holly didn't stop to survey her surroundings. All she knew was that her new coin was getting away from her, and she had just promised Aunt Carrie she would take care of it.

Holly raced after it, completely unaware of the rapidly approaching car heading her way. Robby was watching the whole scenario from a distance, and realized he needed to do something quickly to avoid a catastrophe. He didn't want to fail on his first day on the job.

Mom turned just in time to see the car coming dangerously close to Holly.

"Holly!" she screamed, but Holly's focus was on retrieving her runaway coin.

Robby, flying to her rescue, quickly pulled on the string to Holly's balloon and released it, allowing it to float off into the sky. When Holly realized her balloon was getting away, she stopped and grabbed for it. Fortunately, it was enough of a distraction to stop her as the car whizzed by, narrowly missing her.

Mom and Dad rushed to Holly's side, and she immediately burst into tears. Mom gathered Holly into her arms to comfort her, while Dad retrieved the runaway coin. After Holly had settled down, Aunt Carrie gave her another balloon to replace the lost one, and helped escort the family safely into the car. The three angels once again squeezed in where they could for the return ride home.

As they headed down the road, Robby looked at Gabe, seated across from him on the floor, and said, "How can such a cute little girl be such a handful? I don't think I worked this hard when I was alive!"

"I'm sure you didn't," Gabe smiled back at him.

"That wasn't meant to be a joke," Robby snorted back at him. "I am exhausted!"

"And the party isn't over yet," Daniel stepped into the conversation. "In fact, it's only just begun!"

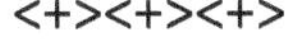

CHAPTER 5
A NIGHT ON THE TOWN

To Robert's good fortune, the remainder of the day proved to be without incident for the Carter family. When darkness fell, Mom tucked Holly into bed, and the rest of the family soon followed suit.

Robby was a bit shaken from the events of the day. Maybe this mission is going to be more work than I thought, he mused to himself. He settled down onto the floor in Holly's bedroom, leaned his head against the wall, and breathed a long sigh. Scenes from today's family gathering played over and over in his mind as he contemplated what he could have done better.

He could have kept the cabinet from toppling, but by the time he realized Holly planned to climb it, it was too late to stop the fall. Plus, if he hadn't been so preoccupied with trying to find his shadow, he could have stopped her from wandering off into the forest and getting so close to the bear. Then as far as the runaway coin incident - well, it had all happened so fast, how could he have possibly foreseen that?

He was feeling like a failure when Daniel and Gabriel drifted into the room.

"What's happening in here?" Gabe asked.

Robby confided in them, sharing how he felt he had failed miserably today.

"What are you talking about, Robert?" Daniel asked. "Your mission is to keep Holly safe, and you did that!"

"But I should have stopped her before she got herself into those dangerous predicaments," Robby argued.

Daniel was not convinced. "Didn't the Father warn us that she was a busy child? Remember how He said she exhausts her parents and constantly stays one step ahead of them?"

Gabe was quick to add, "And this was a successful day, Robby. Everyone made it home safely, even if it was eventful. Just think how it could have turned out if you hadn't been there. Holly had three narrow escapes today, and you rescued her from all of them."

"Yeah, I guess you're right," Robby finally agreed. "Everyone did make if home in one piece, and I guess that is what matters most."

The three paused a moment to reflect, and then Daniel said, "Gabe and I were thinking about taking a walk. We thought it would be fun to get out for a few minutes while the family is sleeping. Do you want to join us?"

Robby glanced quickly at Holly sleeping in her bed and asked, "But what about her? What if she gets up and I'm not here to keep an eye on her?"

Gabe had an idea. "Why don't you just leave your bell at the foot of her bed? If she gets up, your bell will ring as a warning. Then we will all come right back."

It sounded like a good plan to Robert, and he could certainly use a break. So he carefully laid his bell at the foot of Holly's bed, and the trio headed out for a relaxing, evening stroll.

It proved to be a beautiful night for a walk. The moon was shining brightly, and the sky was filled with sparkling stars. A warm, summer breeze blew as the group of heavenly visitors strolled down the concrete sidewalk.

"This is really neat," Gabe said. "I had forgotten how pretty Earth is - the tree lined streets and the big, old houses with their flower gardens in the front yard."

"Franklin is a pretty town, isn't it?" agreed Daniel.

"Yeah, I'm glad I came along," Robby commented. "This is refreshing. It's just what I needed after a day like today. I didn't realize how much work kids can be. This peace and quiet is awesome!"

The trio turned the corner, and there was a dead skunk in the middle of the road. Robby hadn't spotted the skunk yet. His first clue to the skunk's presence came through his sense of smell.

"What is that awful smell?" he asked.

Daniel pointed to the skunk and said, "There's your culprit."

"I had forgotten how bad they smell," said Gabe, covering his nose.

Robby, forgetting the stress of the day, began to let his playful nature show through.

"Guess he forgot to look both ways before he crossed the road," he said.

The other angels chuckled, and Gabe said, "By the looks of him, I would say he took on something pretty big, 'cause he's looking mighty thin!"

The angels laughed again, and then Daniel piped up. "I wonder where his guardian angel was."

Through his laughter, Gabe said, "I don't think skunks have guardian angels, Daniel!"

Robby started to hum a tune, and then broke out into full melody, singing an old tune about a dead skunk found lying in the road. Recognizing the chorus, Daniel soon joined in with rich baritone vocals. Gabriel chuckled, and followed suit, entering into the harmony as well.

By the time the angels reached the end of their song, they were roaring with laughter.

"Aw, man, you guys are good therapy," Robby said. "This is just what I needed. A night out on the town with my best friends - the three of us just having some good, clean fun."

"I don't know how clean it is, Robert," chuckled Dan, as he looked back over his shoulder at the dead skunk. "That guy back there looks pretty messy!"

Looking back, a movement caught his eye. He stopped in his tracks and peered into the darkness behind him. A lone figure passed beneath the streetlight a couple of blocks back.

"Wait a minute, guys," Dan said, turning around to try to catch a better glimpse of the dark silhouette.

The three angels hesitated, waiting for the shadow to draw a little closer.

"Isn't that Joy?" asked Gabe.

"That's what I was thinking, too," said Daniel.

The three angels huddled together, waiting for the subject of interest to draw closer. As she did, it became unmistakably clear that it was indeed Joy.

"Where do you suppose she's going at this time of night?" Gabe asked.

"And all alone, too," added Robby solemnly.

"I'm not sure," Daniel answered, "but I think we better stay close."

The other two angels agreed. Joy drew closer and just before she reached the angels, she crossed to the other side of the street.

"Why do you suppose she did that?" Robert asked. "Do you think she could see us?"

"I'm sure she couldn't," Dan reassured him, "but I think it's time to assume a visible role. She needs some redirection before she gets herself into trouble."

"Whatcha got up your sleeve, Danny boy?" Robby questioned.

"Just a little guidance from an authoritative figure," Dan replied.

Gabe and Robert exchanged raised eyebrow glances.

"This ought to be good," Robby said.

"Okay, Daniel, show us what you've got," Gabe edged him on.

In the blink of an eye, Daniel donned the attire of a police officer, complete with a shining badge and a name tag.

"Very impressive," Gabe grinned.

"Okay, buddy, we're right behind you," Robby encouraged him. "Show us how the big boys do it."

The three angels took flight in an attempt to catch up with Joy, who had continued on her mission down the street. They circled around in front of her to cut her off at the next crossroad. When Dan was in place, the two remaining angels hung back in the shadows to observe. Daniel made himself visible and pretended to be entering from a side street when Joy passed by.

Her glance his way revealed that she could indeed see him. At first she appeared to be distraught at his presence, but seemed to relax a bit when she realized he was a police officer. However, she never broke stride and appeared as though she would pass right by him.

Daniel glanced at the other angels, not sure what to do next. He had expected more of a reaction from her. However, it was obvious she intended to ignore him and continue on her mission.

Gabe nodded his head toward Joy, encouraging Daniel to follow after her. Waving his hands and rolling his eyes, Robby motioned in the same direction. So Daniel quickly headed after her.

"Excuse me miss," he called after her.

Joy glanced over her shoulder to acknowledge his call, but never stopped walking.

Daniel had to lengthen his steps to try to catch up to her.

"Where are you going in such a hurry?" he persisted.

She looked over her shoulder and, seeing that he was catching up to her, she replied, "I'm meeting some friends."

By this point, Daniel had finally caught up and fell into step beside her. The two angels followed close behind, straining to hear the conversation.

"Do you think it's wise for you to be out here alone at this hour?" he asked.

Joy gave a derisive snort and said, "I can take care of myself. And I won't be alone for long. I told you - I'm meeting some friends."

"You never know what can happen out here, especially in the dark hours of the night," Daniel hounded.

Yet, Joy was not convinced that she was in any type of danger. "Thanks for your concern, officer," she said, "but as I said - I am quite capable of taking care of myself."

With that, she abruptly turned the corner and left Dan standing alone in the shadows of the street light. The other angels came to rest beside him, and the threesome stood in stunned silence as they watched Joy continue relentlessly down the road.

"Well, that didn't work too well," Daniel gave a discouraged sigh.

"What should we do now?" Robert asked.

"I'm not sure," Daniel answered. "She seems to be pretty determined about her mission, and I don't know how to stop her. You guys got any ideas?"

Gabe said, "Let me give it a shot." With that, he quickly disappeared.

The remaining couple of angels decided they better stay close to Joy, so they headed down the street in her direction. Just as they caught up to her, the town street sweeper came cruising around the corner. Dan and Robby couldn't help but chuckle when they saw Gabe at the wheel.

"What is he up to?" Daniel asked.

Gabe pulled the street sweeper up beside Joy and hollered out the window to her.

"Kind of late to be out walking alone, isn't it, miss?" he asked.

"What's it to you?" Joy retorted.

"Doesn't this town have a curfew?" he tried again.

"Don't you work for the town?" she asked. "You should know the answer to that yourself."

Joy hadn't stopped walking and Gabe realized she was getting away from him. He struggled to put the sweeper into reverse and, grinding gears, finally managed to back up enough to catch up with her.

"Don't you think you should go home where it's safe?" he called out the window again.

"Don't you have work to do?" she called back, then crossed the road and quickly disappeared down a side street.

Daniel and Robert strolled up beside Gabe, who was sitting in his street sweeper looking very much like a jilted teenager.

"Guess that didn't work well, either," he said.

"What are we going to do now?" asked Robert.

"I haven't got a clue," Dan said, "but we better hurry before we lose sight of her altogether."

Gabe abandoned his street sweeper and the trio rushed to catch up to Joy. When they caught sight of her, they realized she was in trouble. It appeared she was being stalked by a pumped up sports car occupied by a couple of trouble-seeking males. She was doing her best to ignore them, but they seemed resistant to her avoidance and determined to stay close beside her.

The three angels formed an invisible, protective shield around her, and Dan looked questioningly at his buddies. None of them had ever been on a mission like this before, nor had any of them had a teenage daughter to deal with. Daniel was wracking his brain, trying to figure out how to persuade her to return home and rid her of these menaces, but he was coming up blank. What was the solution?

The driver of the car leaned out the window and waved his arm while he called out to her, "Come on, baby, just a short ride. You'll love my set of wheels."

He revved up his engine and added, "It'll be a smooth ride, I promise you."

Joy did her best to ignore him, but he wasn't easily discouraged. As he continued to pressure her, Robert made a motion to the other angels to indicate he had an idea.

The passenger in the front seat leaned forward and, looking past the driver, called out, "We haven't got all night, woman. Are you gonna hop in?"

Robby's eyes got wide and he gave a full-toothed grin as he nodded "Yes." Catching his train of thought, the other angels grinned, too. Robby lifted off the ground and glided seamlessly through the roof of the car, landing directly in between the two men in the front. He turned to look at his angelic friends, smiling from ear-to-ear, as he waved "good-bye" and stomped on the gas pedal.

The driver yelled "What the ...." as the car sped off down the road.

For the first time since her appearance that evening, Joy stopped walking and watched as the car sped away from her and off down the empty street.

Daniel quickly jumped into action and once again donned his police officer uniform.

"Don't you think it's time to head home, young lady?" he asked. "Not everyone out here tonight can be trusted."

Joy spun around to face him. "Oh, you scared me!" she said, looking a bit dazed. "I didn't know you were there."

She paused for a moment, as if contemplating what to do next. She glanced again toward the direction in which the car had disappeared, and then turned to look at Daniel.

"Yeah," she said quietly, "that might not be a bad idea." She abruptly turned her back and began heading in the direction of home.

The angels breathed a sigh of relief and resumed their positions behind her. They lagged back a little, waiting for Robby to catch up with them, but staying close enough to assure they didn't lose sight of Joy. They needed to be convinced that she truly was heading home.

Robert soon joined the group, and the trio broke out with laughter.

"That was very creative, Robert!" Daniel complimented him.

"Yeah, you did alright, my man," Gabe agreed.

Robby strutted proud as a peacock. "Yeah, when I left those two dudes, one had his head stuffed in the engine trying to figure out what had gone wrong. The other had his head stuck down under the dash checking the gas pedal out!"

The angels joked and laughed as they followed Joy down the street, summarizing their tactics of the evening.

"Well, your officer get-up seemed to work well after all," Gabe encouraged Daniel. "And your timing was impeccable. If you hadn't shown up when you did, Joy might have been tempted to continue her flight, even after the scare with those dudes."

"And your street sweeper idea was crafty," Daniel said. "Who else would be legitimately out on the streets at this hour of the night?"

"Oh, that was awesome!" Gabe agreed. "I have always wanted to drive one of those babies. I used to see them out quite frequently in the early morning hours when I was headed to work, but I could never figure out how to get the opportunity to drive one."

"Well, now you have," Daniel smiled.

The angels were only a few blocks from home when Robert's bell began to ring.

"Oh, no, Holly!" Robby gasped. "She must have gotten up and I'm not there to protect her." He turned to look at his buddies and said, "I'll catch up to you guys later. Right now, I have to fly."

He flew as quickly as possible to Holly's room and breathed a sigh of relief when he found her still sound asleep in her bed. Searching around at the foot of her bed, he found his bell on the floor. Apparently, she had just rolled over and kicked it off. Relief flooded over Robby as he realized there was no emergency.

He sunk down into the arm chair in the corner of her room and slowly exhaled. Keeping up with this family wasn't just a mission. It was going to be a real adventure.

CHAPTER 6
COREY CAPERS

Morning dawned, and the Carter household rose to face another day. Mom had made a full Sunday morning breakfast – complete with pancakes, sausage, fresh fruit, and orange juice. As the family dined at the breakfast table, the angels lurked in the shadows.

"Man, that looks good," Robby drooled.

"Makes me wish I was human again. I could definitely handle a big bite of that stack of pancakes," Gabe agreed.

"Keep dreaming, boys," said Daniel. "Those days are over."

Robby gave him a look of disgust.

"Do you always have to be so concrete?" he asked him. "Can't you be a little creative once in awhile?!"

Dan just smiled at him. He knew his angelic friend was just tugging on his wings. Hearing the discussion at the table, he turned his attention to the feasting family. Abigail was apparently trying to convince them that this would be a good day to start a new family routine – attending church together. However, not everyone seemed to be in agreement with her.

"Church is boring," Joy argued. "Besides, I already told Amber that I would go shopping with her."

"And Ryan is coming over to go riding with me," Corey added. "He should be here any minute."

Dad looked sheepishly at Mom. He didn't want to go anymore than the kids, but he wasn't about to admit it. So he simply suggested, "If the boys are here riding their ATVs, then I better stay home, too. They should have an adult around just in case something should happen."

Mom turned her attention to Holly. As always, eager-to-please Holly said, "I'll go with you, Mommy."

"I knew I could count on you, sweetie," Abigail smiled. Since everyone seemed to be finishing up with their breakfast, she suggested, "Why don't you go find a pretty dress while I clean off the table?"

Holly already had a dress in mind, but she was a child who

got easily sidetracked. She watched as Joy grabbed her purse and Corey grabbed his helmet, and they both made their way out the front door. Distractedly, she wandered toward the door behind them.

Joy exited first, calling over her shoulder, "I'll be back around suppertime. We will probably be at the mall for most of the day."

"I'm not going too far," Corey announced, making his exit as well. "We might take a ride up to the mine, but not much further than that."

"You both please be careful," Abby called after her children. "Drive safely and pay attention."

Before disbanding, the angels exchanged glances.

"Looks like I'm spending the day at the mall," Daniel said, rolling his eyes. "I get to hang out with giggling girls who probably want to try on every outfit and pair of shoes they see."

"Sounds safer than my day," Gabriel commented. "I have to try to keep a couple of boys from killing themselves or destroying property with their ATVs."

"Well, what about me?" Robert asked his partners, sounding disgusted. "I get to go to church."

Dan and Gabe looked at each other, then turned back toward Robby and smiled.

"That sounds like a good place for you, Robby," Gabe smirked at his fellow angel.

Dan smiled and nodded his head. "Yes, Robert," he agreed, "you might just learn something new!"

"Thanks for your support, guys," Robby said in defeat. "I think I should have chosen Corey. You know how adventurous I am."

"Too late to change your mind now, buddy!" Gabe said with a smile.

Realizing their cohorts were not waiting for them, the angels quickly rushed outside. Joy had already jumped into her car and was driving out of the yard. Daniel waved a quick farewell, and flew off to catch up with her.

Corey's friend, Ryan, had arrived and both boys were making last minute preparations before heading off on their adventure.

Holly had wandered out to watch, forgetting that she was supposed to be getting ready for church. Gabe and Robby headed out to check on the current status of the siblings.

Holly drifted over to her older sibling and reached up to tug on his sleeve.

"Can I go for a ride with you today, Corey?" she asked, hoping this would be the day he would take her on one of his adventures.

"Not today, sis," Corey replied patiently. "Ryan and I are going up to the mine, and you know Mom doesn't want you up there. Besides, you are going to church with Mom."

"Oh, yeah, I forgot," Holly said, absentmindedly. Turning to head back into the house, she paused and asked, "Can I go next time?"

Although Holly could be obnoxious at times, Corey loved his little sister. Today wasn't the day to baby sit her, though. He had four-wheeling on his mind.

"Yeah, cupcake!" he said, using his nickname for his little sister. Cupcake had been one of her first words, and she had loved them since the beginning. He smiled, thinking about how cute she had been as a toddler, and how sweet she still was. "You can ride next time," he continued his thought. "Maybe Mom will let me take you for a few spins around the yard."

Holly let out a squeal, jumped up and down a few times, and said, "Okay, Corey bear. It's a deal."

Corey grinned down at his younger sibling. "But right now, you better go get ready for church before Mom wonders where you are."

"Oh, yeah," Holly said, as if she had once again forgotten what she was supposed to be doing. With that, she promptly ran into the house to find her favorite dress.

Corey chuckled as he watched her run across the yard. Looking at Ryan, he said, "She's so easy to please."

Ryan sat anxiously on his ATV, full of anticipation for the day ahead. Corey grabbed his helmet and strapped it on, just as charged up as Ryan was.

"Are you ready to ride?" Ryan asked.

Corey revved up his engine and replied, "Am I ever!"

Simultaneously, both boys throttled their ATVs. Perhaps it was to make sure they were running smoothly, or maybe it was just to hear the roar of the engine. To them, it was as sweet as music, with the smoke drifting across the yard a sign of the power they were about to unleash. Yet to Gabriel, it was the sound of fear and dismay, with the cloud of smoke reminding him of a black cloud of doom. Did he have the ability to keep these two thrill seekers out of trouble?

Gabe apprehensively flew over and hopped onto the ATV behind Corey. Giving Ryan a thumb's up, Corey hit the throttle and flew off across the yard.

Watching from the kitchen window, Robby laughed as Gabe reeled backwards, struggling to hang on. As if he had heard the chuckle, Gabe glared back at him. It was almost as though he was daring the other angel to find humor at his predicament.

Corey and Ryan felt as if they were one step from Heaven as they rolled and roared across the open terrain. They found the trail leading up to Miner's Pinnacle, and headed into the woods to follow it to their destination.

Miner's Pinnacle was an old mining pit that had long since been abandoned. All that remained was a quarry, which had filled with water throughout the years and produced some awesome cliffs that thrill seekers liked to dive off. Swimming had not been a part of their plans for the day. Corey loved the thrill of riding his ATV, but even the thought of diving off cliffs was a little overwhelming for him.

It was a beautiful day for a ride. There was not a cloud in the sky, and nothing but pure adventure lay ahead of them. The boys buzzed off down the trail. Neither one was too familiar with the territory, or even sure if they were headed in the right direction. Yet, neither of them was really concerned. This day was made for riding, and that's all they really cared about.

Gabe, being a business man who had spent most of his life sitting in a padded chair behind an office desk, did not share their sentiment. After bouncing around on the back of the ATV and struggling to hang on, he finally decided it would probably be easier to just fly along behind them.

"I guess I'm not much of a country boy," he muttered to himself. "I kind of like the paved roads. We may have had a few potholes to deal with, but they were nothing like these rough, wooded trails!"

However, he knew it was not his place to complain. He had a mission to do, and he intended to do it whole-heartedly. It was just turning out to be at a much faster pace than he had anticipated!

Corey and Ryan did not seem interested in slowing down, no matter how rough or winding the trail became. They weaved in and out, following the trail to the top of the mountain, mostly at full speed. Gabe flew recklessly, dodging branches and fallen trees, trying his best to keep up with them. Finally, at the top of the mountain, they paused to take a rest.

The view was nothing short of spectacular. Below them was a valley of nothing but untainted nature. All that was visible at first sight were lush, green fields dotted with clumps of well-nourished trees and surrounded by a chain of rolling mountain tops. There were very few signs of life below them. Looking intently, one could spot an occasional rooftop poking through the sea of green. To their rear lay the abandoned quarry, full of sparkling, blue water. The clear water seemed to beckon to them.

Turning to face the quarry, Ryan asked, "Want to take a quick dip?"

The trio strode to the side of the quarry and peered over the edge at the water below.

"Ever tried jumping before?" Ryan questioned his friend.

Gabe looked from face-to-face and muttered, "You can't be serious. That's a long way down."

Corey studied the quarry for a moment longer, and then asked, "Do you think it's safe?"

"Oh, sure," scoffed Ryan. "Cameron and Adam were just up here swimming last week. They said it's an awesome jump – as long as you land right!"

Corey wasn't convinced. He liked adventure, but he didn't like pain, and not landing right sure sounded painful to him. He would rather just ride, and he told Ryan as much.

"Let's just ride," he said. "Swimming isn't really my thing."

"Oh, come on – you're just chicken," Ryan scoffed, and proceeded to strut into a chicken dance.

"All right, all right," Corey said. "But just one quick dip and then we ride."

"Fair enough," Ryan agreed.

Gabe groaned. "Looks like I'm going swimming," he thought to himself. He looked over the edge, and suddenly the water didn't seem so crystal clear to him anymore.

"I hope there aren't any bloodsuckers in there," he thought, and then he laughed at himself. "You don't have any blood to suck, Gabriel, so what are you concerned about?!"

Ryan and Corey quickly stripped down to their boxers and walked to the edge. They both stood silently peering over the edge.

"Who's going first?" Ryan asked.

Corey wasn't sure he wanted to go at all, so he said, "It was your idea, so you can."

"That makes sense," Ryan agreed.

Peering over the edge, he studied the situation for a moment, mentally contemplating his departure, style, and method of landing. It didn't matter what he did on the way down, but he needed to be straight as a pencil when he hit the water. Once he had conjectured his strategy, he looked at Corey and said, "Okay, here I go. Wish me luck."

Corey gave him a salute, and Ryan disappeared over the edge. Gabe quickly leapt into action.

"I know I'm not sent to protect Ryan," he thought to himself, "but I can't let this kid kill himself."

Gabriel dove over the edge and caught up with the plunging boy. Ryan's descent was not going as planned. As he approached the water, he looked more like a pretzel than a pencil. Gabe grabbed his ankles and gave him a quick jerk upward, straightening Ryan out just as he hit the water.

Corey stared anxiously over the edge, waiting for his friend to resurface. He held his breath in anticipation, wondering where his cell phone was just in case he needed to call for help. A moment later, Ryan's head popped up from beneath the water, and Corey was able to breathe a sigh of relief.

Looking up at his friend standing on the top of the cliff, a smile broke out across Ryan's face.

"That was awesome!" he called out, stroking the water in an effort to stay afloat. "You gotta try it, man!"

Corey stood on the edge of the cliff, wondering how he could get himself out of this predicament. Gabe stood beside him, trying to come up with a distraction of his own. Corey had absolutely no desire to launch his body off the safety of the ground that he currently stood on, but he knew Ryan would tease him unmercifully if he didn't.

Almost as if he knew Gabe stood beside him, he turned to face him and asked, "What have I gotten myself into?"

Gabe looked back at him and replied, "I was wondering the same thing!"

It was an interaction that held no meaning for Corey, who was totally unaware of the presence beside him. Mustering up his courage, he prepared to take a leap.

"God help me," he whispered, as he plunged off the edge of the cliff.

Gabriel quickly jumped after him.

"I'm not God," he called out to no one in particular, "but I'll do my best!"

Corey's downward fall through the thin air was fast and furious. Gabe was afraid he was going to hit the water too fast. He grabbed at Corey to try to slow him down, but all he could manage to catch hold of was his boxers, and just seconds before he hit the water. He gave them an upward pull, trying with all his might to slow Corey's descent. The thrust did just that, but in the process, the boxers came with him.

Gabe looked down in disgust, realizing he now held an empty pair of boxers in his hand. "Gross," he muttered to himself, and quickly released the boxers to drop them into the water where Corey had last been seen. Then he flew upwards and waited anxiously for Corey to resurface, hoping that he wouldn't have to go beneath the surface into the unknown depths below in an effort to retrieve him.

A few seconds later, Gabe breathed a sigh of relief when

Corey's head emerged. Seeing something in the water, Ryan called out to him.

"What's that floating beside you?" he asked, already suspecting what the answer would be.

"I guess I lost my boxers when I hit the water," Corey explained, hoping if he sounded casual Ryan wouldn't make a big deal of it.

Ryan let out a roar of laughter, which echoed across the mine, seeming to bounce back and forth between the walls of spar as it made its way down to the surface of the water. Corey tried to ignore it as he struggled to retrieve the boxers and casually get them back into place.

Fortunately, Ryan said nothing more of the missing clothing and focused more on the thrill of the dive.

"So, how was your dive, my friend?" he asked expectantly. "Nothing short of awesome?"

Corey didn't particularly consider it to be anything close to awesome, but on the other hand, he didn't want Ryan to think of him as a coward either. So he simply called back, "It was definitely an experience!"

It was a non-committal response. He wasn't denying that it was awesome, but he wasn't admitting he didn't enjoy it either. It had been an experience, and one he hoped to avoid in the future. So, he was quite relieved when Ryan opted to sit in the sun for a bit to dry out before hopping back on their machines. He wondered if Ryan had concerns about jumping again, too, and just didn't want to admit to his fears.

Corey wasn't the only one who was relieved at Ryan's decision. After the two boys had found a place to relax, Gabe lay down on the ground nearby. He was finally able to unwind and enjoy the day. He had forgotten how nice it could be to simply lay in the sun and soak up the peacefulness of nature. However, if he thought it would last, he was only fooling himself. Beside him were two restless boys, and they were anxious to be off on another adventure.

Hearing them stir, Gabe rolled over onto his side and groaned. They were already putting their pants back on, with the intent to head toward their ATVs and retrieve their riding gear. Being restless teenage boys, they weren't apt to sit around for long.

"Come on, boys," he called out to them, knowing they couldn't hear him anyway. "It's a nice day out today. Can't we just stay here a little longer and enjoy the peace and quiet?"

Even if the boys could have heard him, they probably wouldn't have paid much attention. This was a fact that he was well aware of. When it came to riding their machines, there wasn't much that stood in their way.

Knowing there was nothing he could do to stop them, Gabe gave up the thought of relaxation. Seeing they were already well on their way, Gabe charged after them, muttering as he went.

"I didn't know keeping up with teenage boys could be this challenging," he sputtered aloud to himself, glad that no one could hear him. "I thought teenage boys sat on the couch and played video games, and when they went outside, it was to go play ball in the park or go to the library and get a book."

He paused to briefly remember his days with his own children, but then quickly realized the difference. They had been raised in the city, with paved streets and lots of cars. ATVs and dirt bikes were not a part of their world. This country life was something Gabe was not familiar with. He hadn't missed it either, he thought glumly to himself. Realizing the boys were way ahead of him, he dodged a branch as he headed back into the woods to try to catch up with them.

"Out here in the country," he continued to gripe out loud, flapping his wings to fly faster, "you have crazy boys with wild machines that are too fast for them to handle, and no fear of what could happen if they loose control!"

He quickly grabbed a branch and pulled it out of the way, saving Corey from getting struck in the head.

"Just like that," he grumbled away. "Why won't these boys slow down? My wings are getting tired just trying to keep up with them."

The boys stopped at a crossroad in the trail, pausing to decide which way to go. It gave Gabriel a moment to stop and rest as well. He looked at the two ATVs, and called out, "And why do

I have two of them to watch? I only signed on for one! Why am I babysitting for two?!"

There were no immediate answers for Gabe, and the two restless boys weren't waiting around for him to come to any conclusions on his own. They were already off again, heedlessly blazing a trail through the woods. He knew he would need to hurry to catch up with them. When he did, his heart skipped a beat – or so it seemed. However, since he didn't have a heart, it wasn't a possibility.

What he saw was Corey, still sitting on his ATV, but in an extremely precarious position. He had maneuvered too close to the edge of a very steep bank. One wrong move, and both he and his machine would topple over the edge.

Thinking fast, Gabe rang his bell to summon help from his angelic partners. In just a matter of seconds, Daniel and Robert were there to assist him. Daniel was quick to assess the situation and positioned himself on the downward side of the ATV. Blowing hard, he created an updraft to keep the ATV from tipping over toward the edge. The hurricane force breeze propelled Corey backward off the ATV. Gabe quickly reached out to grab him, while Robby seized the opportunity to hop on the ATV and drive it back onto solid ground.

Seeing Corey and the ATV were safe, the three angels collapsed on the ground in relief. As they did, Corey stood up and shook himself off, while Ryan pulled up beside him on his ATV.

"What the heck just happened?" he asked him.

Corey shook his head and said, "I'm not really sure. I got too close to the edge, but after that, everything is kind of a blur."

Ryan said, "All I saw was you on the ground and your ATV driving off without you. I wonder what caused that."

Corey just pursed his lips and shook his head. He had no explanations.

Gabe turned to his buddies and said, "Thanks, guys! That was a close one. I couldn't have done it on my own."

"My pleasure," Robert said. "It got me out of church. I was just as restless as Holly. Sitting still and listening to someone talk has never been my strong point."

"It might have done you some good, though, Robert," Daniel

suggested. "But to be honest, I was glad to come help as well. I was tired of watching teenage girls trying on every pair of shoes in the mall. How can they enjoy stuff like that?!"

Seeing the boys were back on the trail and driving away, Gabe said, "Well, thanks again, but it looks like I better hurry to catch up with them."

"Good luck," Daniel called after his cohort.

Robby watched the two boys flying off down the trail and said, "Man, I should have chosen Corey. Just look how much fun they are having."

Knowing Robby had been pretty wild in his lifetime on Earth, Daniel shook his head and said, "It's probably a good thing you didn't. We would probably spend most of our time rescuing you instead of him."

Robby smiled and said, "Sure, whatever!" He paused, and then added, "I guess I better get back to church now. I don't want to miss anything, you know."

"Listen to the pastor," Daniel called after him. "He might have something to say that you need to hear!"

Daniel chuckled at Robby's perplexed expression, and then added, "Or do you want to go to the mall and try on fifty thousand pairs of shoes?"

Robert waved over his shoulder and said, "I better go. Holly might need me!"

****

Gabe had caught up with the boys, and fortunately, they made it safely back home a short time later. Yet, if he thought his adventures were done for the day, he was sadly mistaken.

Just as he was breathing a sigh of relief, watching the boys remove their helmets, he heard Ryan say, "Sorry we couldn't ride longer. My dad is taking me driving this afternoon, so I have to get home."

Corey thought that was a pretty cool idea. "Your dad is taking you out driving?" he asked his friend. Then he added, "Maybe my dad will take me out, too."

Gabe groaned and said, "Oh, man, just shoot me now and get it over with."

"That won't do any good," he heard a voice behind him state. "You're already dead!"

Surprised that someone had heard his comment, he turned to find Robby headed his way.

"Gonna try the big wheels now, huh?" Robby teased his friend.

"I am not used to boys like this," Gabe admitted. "Mine were city boys who never rode ATVs like these guys, thank God. And now he wants to take the car out."

"Well, at least you didn't get stuck sitting in church all morning," Robby complained. "Like that was fun…"

"It would have been better than jumping off cliffs, careening wildly through the forest, and dangling an ATV over the edge of a bank," Gabe argued. "And now it sounds like I get to go driving with an inexperienced teenage boy. I hope he drives the car slower than his ATV."

"Want me to go for you?" Robby volunteered.

"No, I'll survive," Gabe said. Seeing Holly walking across the yard, he added, "And you had probably better get back to Holly anyway."

Robby looked her way and said, "Yeah, so we can go play dolls, build a tent on Mom's clothes rack, or play in the sandbox."

Gabe smiled, realizing that playing dolls wasn't really Robby's cup of tea. His smile quickly faded when he saw Dad and Corey emerging from the house, with the elder Carter carrying car keys in his hand.

"Uh-oh," he said to his fellow angel, "looks like we're going for a ride."

"Have fun," Robby smiled, then turning to go join Holly, he added, "I'll be thinking of you while I'm building sand castles with Holly. It's gonna be a lot of fun trying to keep the sand out of her cast!"

"Can't you keep her out of the sandbox?" Gabe questioned his fellow angel.

Robby turned and gave Gabe a raised eyebrow look.

"We're talking about Holly Carter here," he said. "She doesn't hesitate to do the things she wants. How am I supposed to change her mind?"

Gabe just shrugged as he headed toward the car. "I guess that's your problem," he smiled back at him. "My problem is about to climb in behind the wheel of the family car."

****

Gabe was surprised at how well the driving experience went. While Corey and Russell sat in the front seat, Gabe lay on the roof of the car where he could have a bird's eye view.

Corey seemed to be doing very well with his driving. Everything was going great until they chanced upon a group of attractive teenage girls walking down the road. All three men became distracted, forgetting the need for someone to navigate the wheel of the car.

Slowing down, Corey stared intently at the girls. Whether he was captivated with their appearance or looking to see if he recognized any of them was not clear. Amusingly enough, the elder Carter on the passenger side was staring just as keenly at the girls as was his younger son. But even funnier, though, was the angel on top of the car. Gabe lay on his stomach, legs bent at the knees with his chin resting on his hand, and he was just as mesmerized by the girls as were the two men inside the car.

So absorbed were the trio with their fascination of the girls, that not one of them was aware of the massive eighteen-wheeled truck heading their direction. Not until he blew his horn and made his presence known, that is. Corey was headed right into his path, and it didn't appear there was time enough to react to avoid a collision.

Gabe quickly flew into action. He leapt off the top of the car and placed himself between the two vehicles. Covering his nose and mouth with his hand, he blew as hard as he could, inflating himself into a giant balloon.

His efforts proved successful, and the Carter vehicle glided off to the side of the road, as the truck breezed past them. Their car came to rest gracefully in the ditch, managing to miss striking anything that would have caused damage to either car or occupant. So smooth was their landing that one might not have even noticed how closely they had come to having a collision.

Fortunately, the Carter men were wearing their seatbelts, and didn't get anything more than a little jolt. Looking around, Dad shook his head and asked, "What just happened?"

Corey glanced around as well, and said, "I'm not really sure."

They turned to see that the truck had continued on its way, apparently unaware of what had just transpired. The group of girls had disappeared as well, probably having stepped inside the store across the road. There didn't seem to be anyone around but the two Carters sitting in their car on the side of the road.

"Well, I think that's enough driving for one day," Dad told Corey. "Let me see if I can get the car out of here, and we'll head home."

They traded positions, and fortunately the car drove out of the ditch with no trouble. Gabe eased himself into the back seat of the car and breathed a sigh of relief.

"Wow, that was a close one," he said to himself. "But I guess that's what I get for watching the girls. I'm too old for this kind of stuff. Maybe I should have traded places with Robby and stayed home to play in the sandbox with Holly."

He thought about the consequences of what might have happened had Robby been here instead of him. He shook his head and said to himself, "No, I guess it was better that I was the angel on duty in this situation."

He paused as he envisioned Robby following the girls off down the street and forgetting the Carter men in the car. He probably wouldn't have even noticed the truck until it was too late to avoid the crash.

"Maybe I was meant to watch over Corey after all," he reasoned with himself. Then he added, "But the next time Robby offers, I might just take him up on it. Keeping up with Corey is taking years off my life – if I still had a life, I mean!"

<+><+><+>

CHAPTER 7
LAUNDRY DAZE

Abigail smiled as she hung her laundry on the rack out in the yard. It was a beautiful, sunny Saturday morning. For a change, the kids seemed occupied and not in need of her attention.

Coming out of the house, Russell was pleased to see his wife looking so relaxed. Her smile seemed genuine, and he wondered what she was thinking about.

"A penny for your thoughts," he whispered in her ear, sneaking up behind her.

She turned to smile at him, and said, "It's just such a beautiful day, and the kids are not nagging me for a change. I enjoy moments like this, because they are few and far between."

He sat down on the swinging glider located on the front lawn, and watched in silence for a moment. He wondered why, after almost twenty years of marriage, that they had never purchased a dryer.

"Would a dryer help?" he asked her.

She glanced up at him, grabbed one of Corey's shirts out of the basket, and turned to hang it on the rack.

"There may have been a time when I would have considered it," she agreed, but then continued her thought. "However, a couple of weeks ago, I had a message in a fortune cookie that changed my outlook."

Russell smirked a bit, wondering how a fortune cookie could alter Abigail's outlook on a dryer. He waited patiently for an explanation.

"The message said 'Take time for yourself,'" Abigail continued. Almost as if she was talking to herself, she proceeded with her rationalization. "At first I laughed about it. I am the mother of three busy children. How could I possibly take time for myself?"

Glancing at her husband, she said, "So, I called Carrie. She knows everything, of course. I felt she could help me figure out how to take time for myself. She told me she had just taken a course that taught how it is helpful to change your mindset. When there are tasks that need to be done routinely, instead of thinking of them as chores, you should think of them as therapeutic."

She looked over at her husband to see if he was still listening to her. Meeting his glance, she lowered the pair of pants she held in her hand and said, "Do you know what I mean?"

He just shrugged, so she gave an example. "Like if you have to walk the dog every night, don't think of it as a chore. Think of it as exercise."

Russell nodded slowly, shrugged, and said, "I guess that makes sense."

"So, that's what I'm doing. I am changing my mindset and viewing the chore of doing laundry a little differently." She smiled up at him and added, "And it seems to be working very well. For one thing, I find hanging the laundry to be very relaxing. And it is one of the few times when the kids leave me alone."

She paused for a moment, and then let out a little chuckle. "Maybe they stay away because they're afraid I'm going to ask them to help. And Heaven forbid they help with chores that are for their benefit."

Russell smiled at his wife. He knew that the kids didn't help out with the chores as often as they should. Yet, on the other hand, if this was therapeutic for Abigail, then he would not push the issue.

Continuing her thoughts, Abigail added, "Plus, it gives me a chance to get outside and enjoy nature. We both know how busy I am inside with all the cooking and cleaning, so it's difficult to get outside and enjoy the fresh air as often as I would like."

"That all makes sense to me," Russell agreed with his wife's logic.

"It's also cheaper than running a dryer," Abigail said. Then, finishing her argument, she added "Plus, the clothes smell so fresh and clean after hanging outside to dry."

"Okay," Russell stated, "you have sold me on why we don't need a dryer. I would buy one to save you the work, but you seem to have come to terms with hanging the clothes outside. But I have another question for you. Why do you put your clothes rack so close to the driveway? I would think you would want it closer to the house."

Abigail turned to survey the yard, and could understand her husband's curiosity. The yard was big enough to allow other options for the rack, but there was one feature that he was overlooking.

"Look up," she said, pointing skyward.

Russell visually traced the direction of her finger and looked upward. Seeing the massive pine tree that hovered over the yard, he came to his own conclusion.

"Aw, you have encountered complications from our family tree?" he surmised.

"You guessed it," she nodded. "If the tree isn't dripping pine pitch, it's loosing needles. And neither one goes well with clean clothes."

"Do you want me to cut it down?" he asked.

Abigail chuckled and said, "Just because it doesn't agree with my laundry? Of course not! I love that old tree."

Abigail smiled at her husband. She loved him dearly for all he did to help make things easier for her around the house. His efforts did not go unnoticed. He was her anchor in life, the force that held her firmly in place when the storms (also known as her children) fiercely rocked her boat.

Just then, Holly opened the kitchen door and called out to her mother.

"Can I make some popcorn, Mommy?" she asked, holding up a bag of microwave popcorn.

"Sure, sweetie," her mother called back to her.

Holly eagerly retreated into the house, happy to have received a positive answer. A moment later, though, she stuck her head back out the door.

"Does popcorn start with 'po'?" she questioned.

Realizing she was probably trying to read the options on the microwave, Abigail smiled and called back, "Yes, it does."

Russell glanced over at his youngest child, then looking at his wife, he asked, "Should I go help her?"

Abigail shook her head. "I don't think so. She has to learn how to do things for herself, and what can go wrong? She just needs to push the popcorn button and wait for the microwave to stop."

Russell shrugged his shoulders and nodded his head in agreement. He had to concur with her on both issues. Hearing someone coming outside, the two parents turned to see Joy exiting the house. She had her purse over her shoulder and was carrying her car keys.

"Are you going some place?" Mom asked her oldest child.

"I'm heading over to Amber's house," she explained. "And I have to stop and get gas at some point. We are going to the mall again tomorrow."

Russell got up from his seat on the swing and walked his daughter to her car. If she was headed to the mall, he wanted to give her car a quick check to make sure he didn't see anything wrong. He circled the car to look at the tires, making sure they didn't need air. When he got to the tire on the front passenger side, he stopped short.

"You're missing some lug nuts on this wheel, Joy," he warned his daughter.

She walked over to stand beside him and realized it was true.

"I wonder what happened to them," she pondered aloud.

"You need to get that fixed right away," Russell admonished his daughter. "especially if you are going as far as the mall tomorrow. I want you to be safe on the road, and missing lug nuts is far from safe."

"I'll take care of it," Joy said sharply to her father, once again feeling offended that one of her parents had to give her instructions.

"You can do it at the garage when you stop for gas," Russell suggested.

"I will, I will," Joy reassured her dad, walking around to the driver side and climbing in.

"Okay, okay," Dad mimicked his daughter.

Abigail had finished hanging her load of laundry, and stood watching the interaction between father and daughter. Aware of her observation, Russell walked over to join her.

"Shouldn't you go with her to make sure she takes care of it?" she asked her husband.

"You were just talking about how Holly needs to learn to

do things for herself," Russell explained, "and Joy needs to do the same. If she is going to own a car, she needs to be responsible and take care of it."

Seeing Abigail's look of concern, he added, "And I will check it later when she gets home to make sure she did."

Abigail smiled at her husband. He was a good man, and a loving father. She was convinced he would make sure their daughter was safe.

Just then, Holly opened the front door and yelled, "Mommy!!"

Hearing her cry of panic, both parents turned and immediately felt alarmed when a wisp of smoke trailed out the door above her head. They ran for the house, not sure what to expect when they got there. Fortunately, it turned out to be a minor problem. Holly had misread the options on the microwave, and had chosen "POTATO" instead of "POPCORN," so her popcorn had cooked much longer than necessary.

"Yuck," said Abigail in disgust. "I don't think there is anything that smells much worse than burnt microwave popcorn."

She ran to open the front door, while Dad opened a window in an effort to air the kitchen out. From their perch in their open airways, both parents watched in stunned silence as Joy put her car into reverse, and promptly back over Mom's rack of clean clothes that she has just hung.

They turned to face each other, mouths wide open and eyebrows raised.

"No way!" Abigail said, running out the door into the front yard.

Russell came running out behind her.

"Harmonie Lane," Abigail called after her daughter, using her legal name. "What did you just do?!"

Heedless of the two annoyed parents behind her, Joy simply drove off down the road. Whether she didn't hear her mother's call, or she just didn't care wasn't quite clear to either of them. And as mad as Abigail was at the moment, it was probably a good thing for both parties that Joy had not stopped.

"Did she do that on purpose?" Abigail asked her husband.

"I hope so," Russell replied.

Abigail looked at her husband quizzically. How could he hope that Joy had backed over the laundry on purpose?

Seeing his wife's bewildered look, he explained, "If she didn't do it on purpose, then that means she was totally unaware of her surroundings. And that doesn't demonstrate very good driving skills."

Walking briskly across the yard to survey the damage, Mom started picking up some of the clothes. Holding up one of Russell's shirts, she turned to face him and said, "Look at the tire mark she left on your favorite shirt!"

Russell rolled his eyes and shook his head in disbelief. Then he joined his wife in checking for damage. He tried to stand the rack back up, but realized he couldn't as one of the legs had been severed.

Holly and Corey had heard the commotion and came out to investigate. Seeing the broken rack and dirty clothes lying on the ground, Corey asked, "What happened?"

"Your sister," Abigail said, as if that explained everything.

Looking at his son through the broken rack that he was attempting to fix, Russell added, "She backed over the clothes rack."

"Seriously?!" Corey grinned. He wanted to laugh, but he could see that his mother was unmistakably upset. He could picture Joy backing over the rack, and wondered if she had burned out on Mom's clean clothes intentionally.

"On purpose?" Holly asked, almost as if she was reading her brother's mind.

"Who knows!" both parents chorused together.

Looking hopelessly at her clean laundry spread across the yard, Abigail decided to take charge of the situation.

"I'll take the laundry back inside and wash it again," she sighed hopelessly. Looking at her husband, she added, "Can you take the rack into your workshop and see if you can fix it?"

Russell agreed that he would see what he could do. He felt confident that he could salvage it.

Looking at Corey, Abby continued, "Corey, can you help your little sister with her popcorn? She pushed the wrong button and burned it. I have a project to work on for your mother, and you know how your sister enjoys your attention."

All parties headed off on their separate missions. Mom grudgingly threw her once clean laundry back into the washer for another round of cleaning. Dad resorted to his workshop to perform magic on the broken rack, and Corey successfully helped his younger sibling with popping a fresh bag of popcorn.

By the time the laundry had finished for the second time, Russell had mended the broken clothes rack. He proudly emerged from his workshop, anxious to show his wife his handiwork. She chuckled when she saw what he had done. The fractured leg now had a metal bracket screwed in place. It wasn't very attractive, but it looked like it would work.

"It's probably a good thing that you are not a plastic surgeon," she said, jokingly. "You didn't do much to improve the look of my rack!"

Russell only shrugged his shoulders. "Well, like you said," he began his argument, "no one ever helps you with the laundry. So you will be the only one that has to look at it!"

****

Russell proved to be right with his philosophy. No one even noticed the dilapidated rack, other than Abigail, since she was the only one who took care of the laundry. As long as the rack did its job, she wasn't particularly fussy about how it looked.

Abigail finished throwing the load of laundry into the basket and headed for the front door. While it had started out a bright sunny day, the sky had clouded over and it looked like rain.

If a shower passes through, the clothes will just get another rinse cycle, she thought to herself. *They could probably use it, after Joy's stunt,* she mused. There were still a few puddles from the rain last night, but if she placed the rack out of range, the clothes should be okay.

She had just finished hanging the last shirt when Corey came out of the house with his helmet in his hand.

"Are you going riding today?" she asked.

Corey glanced up, not realizing his mother was out in the yard. He nodded and said, "Yeah, Ryan's coming over, and we are going for a spin."

"Where are you headed?" Mom inquired.

Corey just shrugged his shoulders and replied, "Not quite sure yet. Probably just circling around the trails in the woods."

Ryan breezed into the yard just then on his ATV. Abigail smiled and waved to him. Then giving her son a quick hug, she said, "Well, you be careful. You're my only son, you know. I want you to come home in one piece."

Corey smiled back at his mom and reassured her. "I will, Mom," he said. Then patting his pocket, he added, "I've got my cell phone right here, so I can call if anything happens."

Abigail smiled and headed for the front door of the house. She was unaware of the three angels coming out the same door. Since Amber had to run chores with her mother, Joy had returned, and was using her laptop in her room. Holly was occupied with playing dolls, so there wasn't much for them to do at the moment. As soon as Gabe saw Corey on his ATV, he let out a groan.

"Not again," he muttered. Then he brightened up and added, "I am not a mechanic, but I did loosen one of his spark plugs. Maybe his ATV won't start and I'll get the day off."

"Don't count on it," Daniel smiled back at his clever friend. "Knowing Corey, he won't quit until that ATV is ready to roll."

Hearing the ATV engine start, Robert smiled and nodded his head. Looking at Gabe, he said, "Yup, you're right. You are no mechanic. It was a good plan, but it didn't work!"

Corey revved up the engine, but something didn't sound quite right. He decided to take a quick spin around the yard first, to make sure everything was in working order, before heading into the forest. As he circled around by his mother's laundry rack, he unwittingly hit a puddle and splashed mud on the newly cleaned clothing.

Still standing on the porch, Abigail watched in horror as her fresh load of white laundry turned a darker shade of muddy brown. She let out an audible groan and called out to her son in anger.

"Corey Michael, look what you did to my laundry!" she yelled after him.

Having decided he was good to go, Corey rode off, following Ryan down the trail that led to the woods. As was the case with Joy, he either wasn't aware of what he had just done, didn't hear his mother calling after him, or he simply didn't care. Riding was all he had on his mind.

Abigail crumpled onto the front steps in a pile of defeat. The angels watched her with sorrowful expressions. As if the muddy clothes weren't bad enough, it started to rain. So, now she would have to bring the whole load back inside.

"Isn't there anything we can do?" Robby asked softly.

Gabe said, "I don't think there is. Our mission is safety for the kids, and there is no safety concern here." Glancing over his shoulder, he could see Corey and Ryan were almost out of sight. "But there is over there, so I better get going."

He quickly flew off to catch up with the two rambunctious boys, while the remaining angels turned their attention back to the defeated Abigail.

"Gabe is right," Daniel agreed. "There is no safety issue here, and God said that property destruction was to take second place."

He paused and thought for a moment, trying to determine a way to lift Abigail's spirits. They had seen how hard she worked for her family, and knew that the kids didn't mean any harm. They were just kids, who didn't always pay attention to their surroundings.

"I've got it," he said brightly, looking at Robert. "Let's give her a rainbow."

Robert smiled at his cohort and nodded his head. Agreeing that it might do the trick, the two angels worked together to produce the right amount of rain and sun to form a brilliant rainbow in the sky. They were pleased with the product, but surprised when Abigail failed to notice it. She was so overcome with despair that she was still sitting on the front step with her head in her hand.

So Daniel caused a gentle breeze to blow. As Abigail looked up, her eyes opened wide at the beautiful rainbow in the sky. She quickly jumped up and opened the front door.

"Girls, come see this beautiful rainbow," she called out to her daughters.

Joy was sitting on the bed in her room typing on her laptop. Instead of running to see the rainbow, as Abigail had expected, she simply muttered, "Big deal. Like I've never seen a rainbow before."

Abigail grimaced and stared at her hopelessly. What had happened to her daughter? Who had stolen her eldest child and replaced her with this ungrateful, snotty, little teenager? However, her mood quickly changed when she saw Holly running her way.

"Quick, before it disappears," she said, and they both ran out the door.

Abigail and Holly stood silently together in the yard, hand in hand, watching in amazement until the rainbow faded.

"That was beautiful, Mommy," Holly said, her eyes still open wide with excitement.

"Yes, it was," Abigail agreed. "And it was just for us, to remind us that there is hope after every storm."

She turned to look at her muddy laundry and said, "And speaking of storms, I have to take this laundry down and wash it again. Your brother just coated it with mud."

"I'll help you," Holly said eagerly.

The two of them went to work removing the soggy clothes from the rack and dropping them back into the laundry basket. However, as they did, Abigail noticed that all the clothes Holly handled were getting even dirtier.

"Holly, what do you have on your hands?" she questioned her youngest daughter.

Holly looked sheepishly at her hands and tried to hide them behind her back, but said nothing.

Abigail realized whatever it was, she was also sporting some of the same residue around her lips, and Abigail now had some on her hands. Finally, Holly reluctantly held her hands up to reveal streaks of chocolate on them.

"What have you been eating?" Mom asked.

"Just a little bit of chocolate," Holly explained.

Mom raised an eyebrow and said, "You had chocolate before lunch time?"

Holly nodded in affirmation, but said nothing more.

Abigail sighed and said, "Well, nothing we can do about it now. Why don't you go wash your hands, and I will finish taking these clothes down."

Holly was quick to comply and ran into the house to clean her hands. Mom looked at the chocolate on her own hands, and impulsively wiped them on her pants. She smiled to herself, thinking with the way things were going, they were just going to get dirty anyway. Then she picked up a few items of clothing and inspected the fresh chocolate stains that had just been applied.

"I am doomed," she muttered to herself. "I am outnumbered three to one. Why don't I just give up now?"

Knowing quitters never win, though, she simply picked up the basket and resolved to go run them through the washer again. As she walked through the kitchen heading for her laundry room, she met up with her husband.

Looking at the basket of laundry in her hands, he asked, "Didn't you just go outside to hang that up? It can't be dry already." He paused for a moment, almost reluctant to ask what had happened.

He thought perhaps the rack he had fixed had somehow failed, but all his wife said was, "Your son," as if that was enough of an answer.

When Corey became "his" son, he knew it couldn't be good, so he followed her into the laundry room.

"Did he knock the rack over like Joy did?" he questioned his wife.

"Oh no, he didn't get near the rack," she smirked. "He just did a fancy little spin out in the yard, hit a puddle, and covered the clothes with mud."

Russell turned away quickly so his wife didn't see his reaction. He could just picture Corey speeding through the yard on his ATV, splashing through a puddle and covering his mother's laundry with mud - and knowing his son, he probably wasn't even aware that he had done it!

"Did he stop to apologize?" he asked.

"Of course not," Abigail said, flabbergasted. "He just flew off into the woods with Ryan like nothing even happened. He must be related to his sister."

Russell nodded his head and said, "I'll talk to him about it when he gets home."

"Good," said Abigail, "because I'm getting pretty tired of washing every load of laundry two or three times! Of course, Holly wasn't much help either," she added. "She had chocolate all over her hands when she tried to help me, so these clothes may not even come clean. Maybe I should just throw the whole load in the trash!"

Russell didn't know what to say to help his distressed wife, so he opted to give her some space. He gave her a quick hug and told her to let him know how he could help as he made his exit and walked away.

By the time the laundry had finished its most recent round of cleaning, Russell had come up with a solution for his wife.

"You know, your laundry doesn't seem to fair too well out in the yard," he told her. "So I was thinking maybe it would be wise to put the rack on the back porch. That way Joy can't back over it and Corey can't get close enough to cover it with mud."

Abigail looked at her husband and smiled. Walking over to him, she placed a quick kiss on his cheek and said, "You are an intelligent man. I think that just might work."

So the back porch became the new resting ground for Abigail's laundry rack. She smiled as she hung her clothes, for the third (and hopefully the last) time to dry. She would outsmart these kids one way or another. While she felt her laundry was safe from Joy and Corey, she would still need to keep an eye on Holly. Not only had she made stains with her chocolate-coated hands, but she liked to use the rack for her tent and frequently knocked the clean clothes on the ground. Maybe if she didn't tell her where the rack was, she wouldn't be able to find it.

Abigail stopped to contemplate that thought for a moment, and then shook her head. No, this was Holly she was thinking about. She was an investigative, inquisitive little girl. She would find the rack in no time, but two out of three problems eliminated wasn't a bad ratio.

******

If Abigail thought she had solved her laundry problem, she was just fooling herself. The next day when she went to check on the status of her laundry, she found it coated with something new. It wasn't chocolate, so she knew it wasn't from Holly. She stuck her finger in it and held it up for a closer look. When she did, she let out with a ferocious growl.

"I can't take it anymore!!!" she screamed.

Her yelling brought her family running. Dad, Corey, and Holly all came to see what was wrong with Mom. Joy was either out, or simply didn't care.

"What's up?" Russell asked his obviously upset wife.

"This!!" she said, holding up her finger with the nasty substance on it.

"What is it, Mom?" Corey asked, leaning over to get a closer look.

"It's bird poop!" Mom said vehemently. "And it's all over my clothes."

All four of them looked up to see the bird's nest located in the rafters above them. Then they almost simultaneously looked at the clothes on the rack which were now spotted with the disgusting stuff.

At first no one said a word, and then Corey started to laugh. Abigail looked at him in disbelief.

"You think this is funny?" she questioned him.

He knew he probably shouldn't be laughing, but he didn't seem to have the ability to stop himself. For some reason, this all just struck him as hilarious.

Abigail was typically a mild mannered person, but the trials with her laundry had pushed her over the edge. Turning to face her son, she said, "Well, if you think this is funny, you can wear some!"

With that, she wiped her poop-stained finger across the front of his shirt and stormed into the house.

Corey looked down at the bird poop smeared across the front of his shirt, then watched wide-eyed as his mother marched away. Looking at his father, he said, "I can't believe she just did that."

Russell felt pure sympathy for his only son. Putting an arm around his shoulders, he said, "You have a lot to learn about women, son. You never laugh until you check their expression. If they aren't laughing, then it would be best if you didn't laugh either – if you know what's good for you anyway. To laugh when your wife is upset usually means a long, sleepless night on the couch."

He patted him on the back and said, "Why don't you go change your shirt. Holly and I will throw these clothes into the machine and wash them again. Then I'll go check on your mother and make sure she's okay."

****

After having thrown the laundry into the washer, Russell went to the bedroom to check on his wife. She was lying on her back on the bed, simply staring up at the ceiling.

"I'm sorry about the laundry," he said tenderly.

She just shook her head and said, "The clothes are going to get worn out from washing them instead of wearing them!"

He chuckled and said, "That might be true."

Reaching over to take her hand, he said, "Is there anything I can do to help?"

She rolled over to face him and said, "I don't know, but probably not. What we have are three totally unpredictable kids, and how do you keep ahead of that?"

Russell nodded his head slowly. She did have a point. It was impossible to stay one step ahead of them when one doesn't know in which direction to head first. Then he thought about a family meeting. Maybe it would help if they at least tried talking to the kids to make them more aware of the dilemmas they were causing.

"I can't do much about the birds, other than taking their nest down," he stated, "but we can have a family meeting and discuss the situation with the kids."

Abigail lay there for a moment and thought about it. Then

she said, "I suppose it wouldn't do any harm. They just need to be more aware of what they are doing and how it affects other people."

"Okay, let's talk about it then," Russell said. He stood up and headed out of the room to call his children to meeting time.

"Family meeting in the living room," he bellowed out.

Once the family was all assembled, he approached the ongoing problem with the family laundry. When he explained how their mother worked hard to hang the laundry on the racks to dry and wasn't being graciously rewarded for her work, Joy spoke up.

"Why can't we just get a dryer like normal people?" she asked.

Dad explained, "Because it is therapeutic for your mother to hang the clothes out on the rack."

"What would be therapeutic for me would be to get away from this family meeting and go hang out with my friends," Joy retorted.

"Oh, sure, Joy," Mom said in a spirit of defeat. "Like your friends are good therapy and a positive influence on you."

Joy gave her mother a grimacing face, but, surprisingly, said nothing more.

Seeing the tension between the two ladies, Dad quickly called the meeting back to the topic at hand.

"What we need to remember," he told them, "is that your mother works hard to make sure we have clean clothes to wear. You need to be more aware of your surroundings when you are outside, and take care to not interfere with her laundry. The reason for this is because it affects you. If you run over the laundry," he paused and looked at Joy, and then continuing, he added, "or throw mud on it," focusing his attention on Corey, "or play in the laundry rack and get food particles on it," he added, turning his gaze in Holly's direction.

Seeing she was playing on the floor and seemingly preoccupied, he continued his thought, "then it is your clothes you might be damaging. And if you stain or ruin your clothing, then that is what you will have to wear until someone comes up with money to buy more."

He looked around at his less than attentive audience. Since Mom's interaction with Joy, their eldest child had sat with her chin on her hand. She kept her attention focused on the floor, being extremely careful not to make eye contact with anyone. Corey had been staring at his cell phone. He apparently had a conversation that he was in the middle of and was anxious to reply. Holly, being Holly, was lying on the floor picking at some imaginary object like it was all that mattered in the world.

Seeing his unenthusiastic audience, he sighed and said, "Well, that's about all I have to say. Pay attention to your surroundings, because what you do in life effects more than just you."

The three children suddenly seemed to return to the element of life. They had apparently been listening enough to know that family meeting was over.

"That's it?" Joy asked.

Dad nodded in the affirmative.

"I'm headed out with my friends then," she announced.

She jumped up and headed for the door. As she walked away, Dad called out to her, "Watch the laundry."

She glanced back over her shoulder and said, "Funny, Dad!"

Corey had picked up his cell phone and was busily texting someone, probably Ryan, making plans for their next adventure.

Glancing up at his parents, he said, "Is it okay if I go over to Ryan's?"

"That's fine," Mom assured him. "Just be safe and remember the rules."

Corey jumped up and ran to get his helmet and riding gear in case they went out riding again. Holly continued to play with her imaginary object on the floor. Mom and Dad stood up and walked out to the kitchen.

Looking at Abigail, Russell asked, "Do you think it sunk in?"

She shrugged her shoulders and said, "Maybe we should have invited the birds. They were in on this, too. Maybe they would have at least listened."

Abigail smirked and then added, "And perhaps have given us a few pleasant chirps before flying off and abandoning us!"

"A chirp would be fine," Russell smiled at his wife, "as long as that's all they gave us when they flew away!"

Abigail looked at her husband and echoed the words of her daughter, "Funny, Dad, real funny!"

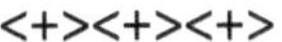

CHAPTER 8
A JOY RIDE

Joy stormed out of the house fuming. She hated family meetings. They always made her feel like a little kid being reprimanded for some foolish childhood mistake, and this time, they were talking about dirty laundry. Just plain idiotic, she thought to herself.

She jumped into her car and tore out of the driveway. Amber would be waiting for her anyway. They had made plans to go to the mall. It was their favorite place to hang out, and Amber had invited some male friends to come along. They were not boyfriends, by any means, but one never knew. Maybe they could become boyfriends, Joy smiled to herself.

Seeing her fly out of the family meeting, Daniel had to do a little flying of his own to catch up with her. He now sat in the backseat of her car, feeling very uncomfortable. He had never liked riding with teenage drivers, even when he had been a teen himself. Currently, he was taking comfort in knowing that he was already dead, so he didn't have to worry about Joy killing him in a car accident.

That's funny, Daniel, he thought to himself. *Maybe you don't need to worry about dying from Joy's poor driving skills, but that isn't your mission here. Keeping Joy safe from her own poor judgment is!*

He settled back and resigned himself to his fate. After all, he had chosen this mission. He had told God himself that he could handle Joy Carter. What he hadn't realized was that it would involve so many crazy trips to the mall, trying on every pair of shoes in each store, and hanging out with giddy, giggling girls. He had never had a daughter, and from his experiences so far, realized he wasn't feeling deprived.

Stop it, Daniel, he reasoned with himself. *This is not all about you. This is about helping Abigail with her challenging children, and Joy is one of those challenges. So stop thinking about yourself and focus here.*

Daniel's pep talk to himself ended about the time Joy arrived at Amber's house. Amber must have been watching for her, because she came out the door just as Joy pulled into the driveway. Daniel groaned when he saw the two boys with her. Having overheard a previous conversation between Joy and Amber, he was aware the two girls would have company today. However, he had hoped for a couple of clean-cut, well-dressed boys. These two goofballs were anything but that. Just observing their behavior, he could already sense trouble. What did two nice girls like Joy and Amber see in guys like this?

After briefly discussing the seating arrangements, it was decided the one named Shane would sit in front with Joy. The other one, Devin, would ride in the back with Amber. Daniel slid into the middle of the back seat and studied the newcomers as they settled in. He wondered if he had what it would take to stay one step ahead of the four of them. "The more" wasn't necessarily "the merrier" in this situation.

As he had dreaded, the trouble began almost immediately. The bag Amber carried with her was not just an oversized purse. It housed a six-pack of beer and a couple packs of cigarettes. Daniel had been warned that these were areas Joy had been exploring, but this was the first time he had to deal with it directly.

"Do you want a beer, Harmonie?" Amber asked her friend. Having known her since kindergarten, she sometimes used her birth name. She knew her family had nicknamed her Joy, but she also knew that sometimes Joy didn't like the reason behind it.

"Harmonie?" Shane questioned, turning to look at Amber. "I thought her name was Joy."

"It is," Amber smiled back at him.

"She has two names?" Devin asked, joining the conversation.

Joy just smirked and explained, "My real name is Harmonie Lane, but my parents nicknamed me Joy. They said that since I became a teenager, I am a real 'joy' to be around."

"Huh, that's kind of cute," Shane chuckled.

Joy gave him a sideways glance and said, "I'm glad you think so. I'm not sure what I think of it. But I guess it's better than Harmonie Lane."

"You don't like Harmonie?" Devin questioned.

"It's not so much the name as it is the reason behind it," Joy explained. She glanced in the mirror and seeing Devin giving her a puzzled look, she continued. "I was a honeymoon baby, and my sick parents named me after the hotel that I was conceived in - The Harmonie Lane Hotel."

"Now that's even funnier!" said Shane, chuckling a little harder.

Joy rolled her eyes and shook her head. She didn't really see the humor in either of the two names. There wasn't much she could do about it, but having him laugh at her situation didn't seem to help much.

"So, Harmonie Lane," Devin addressed her. "What happened to you the other night? I thought you were coming to our party."

Joy thought back to the night she had tried walking over to the party they had invited her to, yet had not arrived at.

"That was a strange night," she recalled. "I started walking over, but kept bumping into people who wanted me to go home."

"Why were you walking?" Shane asked. "You have a car."

"I was worried my parents would wake up if they heard my car start," Joy explained. "So I decided to walk, even though I had never been to your house and wasn't really sure where I was going."

Amber hadn't heard about this adventure. She had decided not to attend the party, and wasn't aware Joy had tried going on her own. She was surprised that her friend would want to go without her, but was curious about the people she had met. "So who kept telling you to go home?" she questioned her friend.

"That was really odd," Joy continued with her explanation. "First, I met a police officer that said it was kind of late for me to be out alone. I never saw a police car, though. He just seemed to be out walking by himself. Then after that, a man driving a street sweeper pulled over to talk to me and suggested I go home. He even backed up to keep talking to me when I didn't stop walking. Just really weird."

"So what made you decide to go home?" Devin asked.

"To be honest, I got a little scared," Joy admitted. "A couple of guys pulled up beside me and wanted me to go for a ride with them."

"How did you get away from them?" Amber asked, concerned for her best friend.

"That's the really freaky part," Joy said, picturing the car suddenly flying off down the road. "They just drove off down the road. It was almost like they weren't in control of the car and didn't know what was going on. Just totally bizarre."

"Well, I'm glad those men, whoever they were, seemed to be looking out for you," Amber admonished her friend. "You shouldn't have been out walking alone at night."

Wanting to change the subject, Joy said, "Yeah, I'll take one of those beers now."

Daniel knew that Joy shouldn't be drinking, especially since she was driving. He had to do something to try to stop this situation. So, after Amber opened the can and tried to hand it to her friend, Daniel bumped her arm and knocked it out of her hand. The can took a sharp right, and landed directly in Shane's lap.

"Whoa, that is cold!" he yelled sharply. He grabbed the can to upright it, but not before it had left a puddle in his lap.

"Now I look like I wet my pants," he said grumpily.

"Yeah, and you're gonna smell like a brewery while we're at the mall," Devin chuckled.

"There are some napkins in the console if you want to try to dry yourself off," Joy suggested.

Shane quickly grabbed a handful of napkins and started dabbing at his soggy pants. When he decided he had done all he could, he said, "Well, that's gonna have to be good enough. I'll just have to stay away from the security guards so they won't get a whiff of me!"

There were still five cans of beer left, and Daniel knew it would be challenging to keep Joy from connecting with one of them. The next can Amber offered to her, he knocked over so that it spilled on the floor.

"Nice!" muttered Joy. "Now my car is going to smell like a brewery. How am I going to explain that to my parents?"

"That's easy enough," Shane smiled at her. "Don't let them get in your car."

Joy glanced over at him, not sure if she was impressed with

her front seat passenger. He seemed to be pretty simple-minded. How exactly could she keep her parents out of her car? It wasn't like it would air out overnight. What if her dad opened the door a couple of days from now? It would still stink. Maybe she could leave her car at Amber's house and pretend it wouldn't start.

Joy told Amber to just pass her an unopened can, and she would open it herself. However, when Joy tried for her third can of beer, it slipped through her grasp and rolled across the floor. Joy finally decided it wasn't meant to be.

"Never mind," she said impatiently. "I will just wait until later to have a beer."

Daniel breathed a sigh of relief. He had conquered the challenge of keeping Joy from drinking and driving. If he thought the battle was over, though, he was sadly mistaken. Once the beer issue was resolved, the pack of cigarettes came out.

"Teenagers!" Daniel growled to himself. "Why are they so determined to abuse their bodies?!"

Devin opened the pack of cigarettes and leaned forward to give one to Shane. When he did, Daniel quickly pushed the pack across the seat. When Devin sat back, he landed right on top of them.

"Devin!" Amber shouted, "You just sat on top of the whole package. You probably crushed them."

Devin pulled the pack out from beneath him and investigated it. "A couple of them didn't fair too well," he said, pulling out a couple of bent cigarettes, "but we can still use them."

Daniel was not as successful fighting the cigarettes as he had been with the beer. So, he decided to take a different approach. Realizing the radio was turned on, he decided to use it to help him in his task. He would make his own advertisement to try to catch their attention.

"Smoking is hazardous to your health and can cause lung cancer," he blasted through the car speakers. "But help is available. Contact your local health center and sign up for a smoking cessation class today. Don't let a habit control the quality of your health. Act today."

He was no advertising salesman, but he thought he hadn't

done a half bad job. Before he could pat himself on the back, though, Joy reached over and switched the radio station. He wasn't sure if he had stirred a spark in her, or if she felt his ad didn't apply to her. Either way, she didn't seem interested in listening to what he had to say.

Dan sighed in defeat, and sat back to contemplate his next approach. As he tried to recall some of the methods they had used in his lifetime as a drug and alcohol advocate, he realized they had a bigger problem at hand. Something wasn't right with Joy's car. There seemed to be a shimmy or wobble going on. Something was definitely wrong.

He decided to take an inspection of the car to see if there was anything he could do to help. It was a challenge to do an external inspection of the car when it was going about 70 mph down the highway, but he finally determined the problem was with the front passenger side wheel. Daniel had overheard the conversation between father and daughter about the missing lug nuts, and having followed Joy around for the last few days, he couldn't remember her having replaced them. Now it looked like they were in danger of losing the front wheel all together, as the few lug nuts that remained were coming loose.

Daniel measured his options, and came to the conclusion that there weren't many. He had to keep the wheel from falling off, one way or another. So he assumed a fetal position and welded himself to the front wheel of Joy's car. If he had to become a lug nut to keep Joy safe, then he would be the biggest, strongest lug nut ever.

Although he had never been a fan of amusement park rides, he would have given anything to trade his current situation for a roller coaster ride. At least he would be strapped in, and the ride would be short-lived. Traveling as a huge lug nut on the tire of a car driven by an out-of-control teenager came with no guarantees. He could only hope that they were almost to the mall. They couldn't get there soon enough, as far as he was concerned.

At last, after what seemed like just short of forever, they pulled into the parking lot of the mall, and Dan collapsed onto the ground. His head was still spinning and he couldn't focus on anything, but at least they had arrived safely. As the world spun above him, he silently prayed that the occupants of the car would take their time getting out. Unfortunately, it was to be an unanswered prayer, as they all seemed anxious to exit. He probably would have felt the same way, had he been in their shoes.

Shoes, he groaned to himself, *time to go try on some more shoes! I can't wait!* Yet, as he lay on the ground with his head still spinning, he decided watching giddy girls trying on shoes wasn't as bad as what he had just experienced.

Since the two couples were not waiting for him, he decided he had best get off the ground and follow them. He had to do something with Joy's car before he left, though. There was no way he was riding all the way back home as a lug nut again. So he reached over, from his seat on the ground, and slowly let the air out of her tire.

There! he thought successfully to himself, *I guess she's not going anywhere now.*

Seeing the teenagers had almost reached the entrance of the mall, he quickly flew after them. Or he tried to fly after them, that is. He more likely resembled a pinball as it bounced from wall-to-wall, making its way down through a pinball machine.

This must be how Gabriel feels when he is chasing Corey through the woods, he chuckled to himself.

****

As it turned out, he actually enjoyed his time at the mall today. After such a wild ride in, he was thankful that the girls took their time shopping and checked everything on the racks. Daniel didn't know if his head would ever stop spinning, or if he would ever feel normal again.

Walking down the main corridor of the mall, the two couples came upon a photo booth.

"Let's do a group photo," one of the boys suggested.

Joy and Amber thought it sounded like fun, so they quickly agreed. Daniel sat back to watch, wondering how all four kids were going to fit into the booth. It was a tight squeeze, but they somehow managed to get all four heads into the picture. The fun began when they decided to take turns with single shots.

"Amber's turn," Devin called out, so three heads ducked while Amber posed for her photo shot.

After her photo was done, Shane said, "Okay, Joy, now it's your turn."

The other three ducked, or stuck their heads out of the curtains, so Joy could have her single shot. Daniel couldn't help but chuckle at their antics. Maybe these boys weren't so bad after all. It appeared they had a sense of humor.

When the couples had finished with the photo booth and were satisfied with their pictures, they continued with the exploration of the mall. They took a lunch break in the food court and then, finally, after the girls had tried on what seemed like every pair of shoes and checked every piece of clothing on all racks, they decided it was time to head home.

Upon reaching the car, Shane was the first to notice the flat tire.

"Looks like we're not going anywhere any time soon," he announced, pointing to the tire.

"What happened to my tire?" Joy questioned, stepping over to get a closer look.

Devin bent down to investigate and asked, "What I would like to know is what happened to your lug nuts? We're lucky the wheel didn't fall off on the highway!"

"Oh, no," Joy groaned. "My dad told me to stop at the garage and get that taken care of, but I forgot."

The group of four looked at one another, but no one was quite sure what to say. Visions of what could have happened on the highway were circulating through their minds, and they were far from pleasant thoughts. Finally, Amber spoke up.

"So, what do we do now?" she asked quietly.

"Do you have a spare tire?" Devin asked.

"I do," Joy answered, then added, "but not any spare lug nuts."

While the teenagers tried to determine what to do, Daniel

sat on the top of the car relaxing. When it came to keeping up with Joy, there weren't a lot of opportunities to sit back and unwind. Whatever they came up with for a solution, he was going to make sure it was a safe one before they hopped back onto the highway. There was no way he was going to spin himself silly as he hugged the front wheel on the return trip home!

"Why don't we just call your dad to come help us?" Amber finally suggested.

"And admit that I forgot to get the lug nuts for the front tire?" Joy said in exasperation. "He would probably take my car away."

Looking at Shane's stained pants, she added, "Plus, Shane and my car both smell like a brewery. I don't want my father to catch wind of that."

"Okay, I've got it," Devin said. "Let's just go over to the automotive store across the road and buy some lug nuts. Then we'll put the spare tire on, and we should be good to go."

So they decided Amber and Devin would go for lug nuts, while Joy and Shane worked on taking the flat tire off. At first, Daniel was content with reclining on top of the car and enjoying the beautiful day. However, watching Shane with the car jack, it was soon obvious that he didn't really know what he was doing. He decided he had better help him out before the situation got worse. So he slid down off the top of the car to help stabilize the front end, while they waited for Devin and Amber to return and secure the spare tire safely into place.

Soon the new tire was on with all lug nuts in place. Daniel gave it a final inspection, and then settled into place in the back seat with Amber and Devin. It had definitely been an adventurous day. If Gabe thought he had it rough chasing Corey through the woods on his ATV, then Daniel had a story to compete with his. Thank goodness they didn't have to worry about property damage, too. Keeping these kids safe was proving to be all the three angels could possibly handle.

Daniel leaned back and breathed a sigh of relief. He knew they weren't home yet, and it was still his mission to make sure they arrived safely. Yet on the other hand, there were two less things to worry about. The front wheel now had adequate lug nuts in place, and the beer was gone.

As they traveled home, he thought back to the day far above when God had introduced the Carter family at meeting time. He chuckled to himself when he remembered thinking that this sounded like the perfect mission.

Either kids are more challenging these days, or I have forgotten what life is really like, he smiled to himself.

Whichever the case may be, he decided he would take a Sabbatical when he got back to Heaven, and not volunteer for any further missions for awhile. Floating peacefully on a fluffy, white cloud surrounded by heavenly beings playing harps sounded just fine to him right about now!

<+><+><+>

CHAPTER 9
HEAVENLY HOLLY

"Family meeting, kitchen table," Dad called to his three children. It was Columbus Day weekend, but the weather had been unseasonably warm and Mom was still able to hang the laundry outside. Seeing her depart through the back door with a basketful of laundry, Russell wanted to use the time to conspire with his children.

He was hopeful that they would come quickly, since he knew he had a limited amount of time. Abigail liked to take her leisure while hanging the laundry, but there were only so many clothes in a basket. He hoped to have business taken care of before she reached the bottom, so he was pleased to see his children respond quickly to his call.

Sitting down at the table, he wasted no time getting to the point. "So tomorrow is your mother's birthday," he reminded them.

They all nodded their heads in agreement, wondering what he might have up his sleeve this time. He had always made it an annual event, sometimes showering their mother with gifts, flowers, or even a special trip. They were eager to know what the plan was for this year.

"I thought in the morning we could start with breakfast in bed," he suggested.

"I can make Mommy some toast," Holly offered enthusiastically.

"Sure you can, sweetie," Russell smiled at his youngest child. "And I can make her some eggs to go with the toast."

Corey wanted to do his part, so he offered, "I'm probably not the best at making coffee, but I'll try to brew a pot for her."

"That sounds good," Dad was pleased to see his children's willingness to give their mother a special treat for her birthday.

Since he hadn't heard any input from Joy, he looked her way and was instantly disappointed to see her playing with her cell phone.

"Joy, you know the rules," he reprimanded her. "No using

cell phones during family meetings. You'll just have to put it away for a few minutes."

She rolled her eyes in annoyance and set her phone on the table, but she still didn't seem interested in becoming involved with the family planning in progress. So Dad gave her a little prompting.

"And what will you do for Mom tomorrow?" he questioned.

Joy just shrugged her shoulders and said, "I'll think of something."

"Okay," Russell nodded, giving his daughter the benefit of the doubt. "You think about it and see what you can come up with. Maybe you can cut up some fruit to make her breakfast a little more special."

"Yeah, sure, whatever," Joy replied, noncommittally. Looking around the table and seeing everyone looking her way, she asked, "Is that it? Are we done here?"

Russell knew family meeting had never been one of Joy's favorite times, but he still hoped deep inside that she would become a more active part of this family. Knowing that they had covered breakfast for tomorrow, he only had one more item to add.

"After breakfast, I was thinking about taking your mother to the beach for the day," he added. "Do you think you guys can find someplace to go for the rest of the day?"

"I'm sure Ryan will let me hang out at his house," Corey offered.

Looking at Holly, Dad smiled and said, "Maybe Aunt Carrie will let you come for a visit."

Holly grinned and bobbed her blonde head up and down. "I love to go to Aunt Carrie's," she stated. "I hope she says I can."

"I'll give her a call," Dad said.

Turning to see if Joy had a plan, Russell was surprised to see her looking at him with a questioning expression on her face.

"Joy?" he asked, raising an eyebrow and returning her questioning gaze.

"Well," she started, "I was wondering if I could invite Amber over, and we could just hang out here tomorrow."

Russell pursed his lips as he contemplated her request. He wasn't sure he wanted two unsupervised teenagers loose in his house when he wasn't present, yet he wanted to think he could trust his oldest daughter. She was close to being an adult and would be graduating soon. She would be on her own at college next year, so perhaps he should allow her a little freedom, and the opportunity to prove herself.

"What would the two of you do all day?" he asked thoughtfully.

Joy shrugged her shoulders and said, "I don't know, really. Probably just watch TV and play on our laptops."

Russell thought for a moment longer, and then decided to grant her request.

"Okay, but with some restrictions," he finally stated. "Amber's parents have to be in agreement, plus no boys, no beer, and no company other than Amber."

Joy's eyes flew open wide. She hadn't expected him to go along with her plan. She had been prepared to make another dramatic exit for not getting her way. So she nodded her head enthusiastically and smiled.

"And you keep in touch with us," Dad added. "Mom will have her cell phone, so you let her know if everything is okay. I know you are almost an adult, but 'almost' doesn't count. You are still our responsibility, and I don't want any repercussions from giving you some space."

"That's not a problem, Dad," Joy reassured him. "We will behave ourselves and treat the house with respect."

Looking out the window and seeing that Abigail was finished with the laundry, Russell quickly said, "Well, that about covers it then. Your mother is coming, so family meeting is dismissed."

Before splitting up to follow their young subjects, the angels had a brief conversation.

"I wonder if Aunt Carrie has closed up her pool," Robby pondered aloud. "Maybe I can hang out there tomorrow."

"And who will keep an eye on Holly?" Gabe asked.

"Aunt Carrie," Robby chuckled.

Daniel and Gabriel chuckled at Robby's humor, and then considered their own plans for the day.

"Sounds like I will be on another mission to keep Corey

and Ryan from killing themselves," Gabe moaned. "But maybe the terrain at Ryan's house won't be so bad. Or maybe, if I'm in luck, they will want to play video games instead of riding their ATV's. I could use a break."

"Yeah, and what about me?" Daniel asked. "I can't believe Russell agreed to let Joy have the house to herself. She will probably invite the whole neighborhood over and have a wild party."

The other two angels only nodded in agreement. Knowing Joy, she was capable of anything, and she did like to party.

"Guess we better make sure we have our bells with us," Gabe suggested. "Sounds like you might need some help."

"I wish I could just go to the beach with Mom and Dad," Daniel sighed. "I could use a day of relaxing in the sun."

"But that is probably why we are here," Robby suggested, "because Mom and Dad are the ones that need the break."

Daniel and Gabriel looked at Robert with surprise. He wasn't usually the one who had things in perspective.

"Wow, Robert," Daniel said in amazement. "Sometimes you surprise me."

"Yeah," agreed Gabe. "I didn't expect the fun-loving, anything-goes angel to be the one to remind us of our mission."

Dan and Gabe patted him on the back as they headed off to catch up to their child.

"Good job, my man!" Daniel smiled, flying off in Joy's direction.

"Ditto!" added Gabriel as he headed off to find Corey.

****

As soon as Mom walked through the door, after having finished hanging the laundry, Holly greeted her with a request.

"Can I make some cupcakes for your birthday tomorrow, Mommy?" she questioned.

Abigail was surprised that Holly would remember her birthday, and was immediately suspicious.

"How did you know tomorrow was my birthday?" Abigail

asked her youngest child, who simply looked up at her mother with wide eyes and a look of surprise.

Instantly concerned that she would give the family plans away, Holly quickly recovered and said, "Daddy told me."

"Oh," Abigail replied, satisfied with her answer. Then thinking about Holly's request, she said, "I don't think I have any cake mixes."

Holly was always swift in coming up with an answer. She may have been impulsive, but there was nothing wrong with her problem-solving skills.

"We can go to the store and buy one," she offered.

"You want to make cupcakes instead of a birthday cake?" Abby asked.

"Of course!" Holly replied emphatically. "Corey bear calls me cupcake, so that's what I want to make!"

Mom smiled and decided Holly's logic made sense. Given that she didn't have a lot of plans for the day, she decided they could take a trip to the store to buy a cake mix. If Holly was thinking of someone other than herself and wanting to do something nice for them, she would do all she could to support that. She would make an extra effort to keep her that way as long as possible, with her focus on other people's feelings rather than being wrapped up in her own, like her older sister seemed to be lately.

"Okay, we can go to the store," Mom agreed, which promptly brought a smile and squeal of excitement from Holly. "Just let me tell Daddy what we are doing, and I will be right back."

Abigail went to find her husband to let him know they were heading to the grocery store.

"I was thinking about doing a barbeque for supper tonight in honor of your birthday," Russell told his spouse. "Do you want to get some burgers and hot dogs while you're there?"

Mom paused and thought about it. She really didn't have time for a cook-out, but yet she didn't want to miss the opportunity for some family time. She knew Joy and Corey would soon be heading off to college, so times like these were limited.

"I am way behind on the laundry," she began. "I did a load of dark clothes today because I knew Joy would have a fit if she didn't have her favorite jeans for school on Tuesday, but I still have a couple more loads to do. The whites always take a long time to hang up...all those little pieces, you know, like socks and underwear."

Dad cocked his head and raised an eyebrow. "So, what would you rather do - have a cookout with your family, or work on dirty laundry?"

"Yes, you're right," Abigail agreed with him. "Family time should always come first. So, Holly and I will pick up everything we need while we're at the store. Maybe I can get the whites washed tomorrow."

For a moment, Russ thought about telling her that he had plans for the beach, but then he decided against it. He wanted it to be a surprise, so he would just spring it on her tomorrow after her breakfast in bed. That way she wouldn't have time to come up with any excuses for not going.

Mom went to find Holly, and they headed for the car. Holly climbed into the backseat and automatically put her seatbelt on, then picked up a book she had left sitting on the seat. Robby climbed in beside her and jokingly wondered to himself if he should put his seatbelt on, too.

As they started to back out of the yard, Mom realized her view down the road was obstructed by a temporary road sign. Since Holly was in the backseat, she thought she might have a better view of the road.

"Are there any cars coming, Holly?" Mom asked.

Holly glanced down the road, uttered a negative reply, and then went back to looking at her book. Robby could clearly see that a huge truck was heading their way, and couldn't understand why Holly hadn't warned her mother. Knowing that he had to do something fast, he made the distant sound of an air horn to catch Abigail's attention. Fortunately, it worked, and she stopped quick enough to miss an impact with the fast moving truck.

"Holly!" Abigail said, flabbergasted. "I thought you said there was nothing coming?"

Holly looked up at her mother with a surprised expression and said, "You asked if any cars were coming. That wasn't a car, Mommy, it was a truck!"

Abigail could only shake her head in disbelief and wonder if she was going to survive all eighteen years of that child's life!

****

When they got to the store, Abigail decided to get some fruit to have with their burgers.

"Can I get some strawberries?" Holly asked.

Abigail turned to find Holly investigating the berries. She decided a fruit salad to go along with the burgers tonight sounded like a good idea. So she told Holly to not only grab some strawberries, but some cantaloupe, grapes, and blueberries, too. If Abigail thought that Holly would be satisfied with fruit, though, she was only fooling herself. They proceeded on to the bakery department to pick up some rolls, and Holly asked for some cookies.

"No, Holly," Abigail replied. "We don't need any cookies."

"But I love cookies, Mommy!" Holly insisted.

Abigail stood firm. Holly didn't need cookies.

In the snack food aisle, Mom stopped to pick up some potato chips. Holly was not satisfied with one bag of chips, though.

"Can we get barbecue chips, too?" she asked

Mom responded with, "No, Holly, the goal is not to see how much money we can spend. We are only here to pick up a few things for the cookout and a cake mix, remember?"

When they passed the beverage section, Holly thought for sure they should buy some soda. Once again, Abigail replied with a firm, "No!"

When Holly whined, she added, "We can make some iced tea when we get home."

She was beginning to wonder why she had brought Holly along with her. She knew how difficult it was to shop with her to begin with, frequently having to deny her numerous requests, and often finding things in her cart at the check out counter that she hadn't intended to buy.

It would have been quicker, easier, and even cheaper to just run to the store by herself to get the cake mix. Stopping to take a survey of the items in the cart, she decided they had everything they needed, and no extra things that Holly might have slipped into the cart. She decided she might as well grab a gallon of milk while they were there and then check out.

As she looked for a gallon of milk in the cooler, she vaguely heard Holly questioning her again. Holly's constant nagging was starting to wear on her, and she was ready for this adventure to end. She had had all she could take of her persistent requests, and was not about to give into her now, when they were so close to being done with the task.

"Isn't that Aunt Carrie?" Holly asked her mother.

No longer processing Holly's inquisitions, Abigail automatically replied, "No, Holly."

Straining a little harder to see the subject coming down the aisle, Holly insisted, "I think it is, Mommy."

At the end of her rope, Abigail grabbed the gallon of milk out of the cooler and replied, "I said 'No,' Holly, and I mean it!"

By then, Aunt Carrie had spotted them and was making her way over. Seeing the look on Abigail's face, she said, "Are you having a bad day?"

Holly looked at her aunt and smiled, then turned innocently back toward her mother and said, "See, Mommy, I told you it was Aunt Carrie!"

Abigail turned to face her sister and rolled her eyes.

"Even a simple trip to the store to buy a cake mix can be exhausting," she told her.

"I can relate to that," Carrie agreed. "I do have a few children of my own, you know." She smiled at her sister and added, "But Russ just called me about tomorrow."

Other than tomorrow being her birthday, Abigail wasn't aware of any other plans. She looked questioningly at Carrie and asked, "What about tomorrow?"

Carrie wasn't sure if she should say anything more. She had assumed, since Russell had called her, he would have told Abigail of his plans to take her to the beach. If it was supposed to be a surprise, she didn't want to spoil it, but Holly quickly came to her rescue.

"Daddy wants to take you to the beach," she spoke up. Looking at Aunt Carrie, she added, "and I'm going to Aunt Carrie's house for the day!"

"Yes, you are," Carrie smiled down at her niece. Giving her nose a friendly little tweak, she added, "and we are going to have a good time. Uncle Ted is already making plans about what we can do."

"Like what?" Holly asked.

"Like you will just have to wait and find out," Aunt Carrie grinned in return.

Looking her sister's way, she added, "And Mommy and Daddy can relax on the beach while we are having our own fun."

As she turned to walk away, she said, "I'll see you in the morning."

"Thanks, Carrie," Abigail called after her. "I really appreciate it."

"Not a problem," Carrie called back over her shoulder.

Turning back to Holly, Abigail said, "Well, we better head home so we will have time to make our cupcakes and fruit salad before the barbeque."

As they made their way back down the snack aisle, Holly spotted some trail mix.

"Oh, Mommy," she called out. "I love trail mix. Can I have some?"

Abigail had determined that she wasn't going to give into anymore of Holly's requests, but she was feeling better after her conversation with Carrie. Trail mix was nutritional and if it would make Holly happy, then why not get it. Plus, maybe it would keep her occupied and quiet in the car on the ride home.

"Sure, honey," Abigail agreed. "Go ahead and grab some."

Realizing she had a headache, possibly from Holly's merciless nagging, Abigail decided to take a quick stop in the Health and Beauty Aids aisle to grab some pain relief medication. While she was trying to determine which one to buy, Holly wandered off down the aisle.

"Look at this, Mommy," she said, coming back with a small box in her hand. "You should have bought this for your car."

Abigail couldn't figure out how anything in the Health and Beauty Aids aisle could be useful for her car, so she was curious as to what Holly had found.

"What is it, sweetie?" she inquired.

Holly was studying the package and didn't respond.

"Why do you think I would need that for my car?" Abigail asked, reaching over to take the package Holly was holding out to her.

"Cause it is Fixodent," Holly replied.

When Abigail looked at her quizzically, Holly added, "Remember when Corey hit your car?"

Mom nodded, waiting for Holly to explain.

"So this is Fix-uh-dent," Holly sounded it out. "You could have used this to fix the dent Corey made instead of paying the garage all that money!"

Abigail had to hide her smile. She didn't want Holly to think she was laughing at her, but she did seem to have some practical problem-solving skills!

****

Russell greeted them in the driveway and helped carry the groceries into the house. Abigail was disappointed when she looked into the backseat of her new car and realized Holly had spilled the trail mix. She decided to make the cupcakes so they could get them into the oven, then she would come out and vacuum the car while they were baking.

Holly and Abigail had a great time baking together. As they worked, Holly chatted her mother's ear off. *Maybe she does talk a lot*, Abigail thought to herself, *but at least she is pleasant. I hope she always keeps her upbeat attitude.*

They put the cupcakes into the oven, then seeing that Holly was covered with cake batter, Mom suggested she go take a quick bath while she went to clean her car out. When she saw Joy sitting on her bed, she called to her and asked if she could keep an eye on the cupcakes while they baked, and check in on Holly in the bathtub. Without looking up from her laptop, Joy called back that she would.

Holly headed for the bathroom while Abigail grabbed the vacuum and headed out the door. Robby decided to allow Holly some privacy, so he remained by the closed door where he could still hear the activity inside. After Holly had finished running the water, Robby could hear her splashing in the bathtub.

He sat down and leaned against the door, enjoying the smell of the baking cupcakes and wishing he could be human again long enough to take a bite of one of them. He felt the bathroom door vibrate and at first thought Holly was coming out, but then he realized it was just repercussion from movement inside the bathroom. It sounded like Holly had just closed the closet door.

A moment later, he heard a humming noise. Not wanting to invade on Holly's privacy but concerned about what was happening, he peaked his head inside the door to take a look. He wanted to scream when he saw Holly sitting in the bathtub blow drying her hair!

Yikes, what can I do?! his mind screamed. *She's going to electrocute herself!*

Not realizing the predicament that Holly was in, Abigail was busily vacuuming her car. It had been awhile since she had cleaned it, so she decided she would just vacuum the complete interior. She started in the front and worked her way around to the backseat where Holly had been sitting. She chuckled when she got to the door where Holly had been. There was not just a pile of trail mix on the floor, but also on the driveway leading away from the car.

Abigail smiled to herself. "Well, it is trail mix," she said out loud, "and I'm not surprised that she left a trail!"

She surveyed the situation for a moment, trying to figure out the easiest way to clean it up. Looking at the vacuum hose in her hand, she finally decided the quickest way was to just vacuum it up. What she didn't realize was that Joy was watching her from inside the house. Having come out into the kitchen to check the cupcakes, she looked outside to see what her mother was doing.

"Okay, now I've seen everything," Joy called out to her

father, who was relaxing in his recliner in the living room while watching television.

From his perch, he could see Joy staring intently out the window. "What's happening?" he called back.

"I think Mom has finally gone nuts," Joy stated. Turning to look at her father, she added, "She's vacuuming the driveway!"

Russell had to come see for himself. He hurried out to the kitchen and joined Joy at the window. Sure enough, there was Abigail busily vacuuming the driveway.

Continuing to stare out the window, he said, "You're mother has been under a lot of stress lately. I was hoping a day at the beach would help save her sanity, but maybe I'm a day too late!"

They were so intent on watching Abigail vacuum the driveway that Joy forgot all about checking the cupcakes. Neither one of them had noticed the humming noise coming from the bathroom, either, nor had they thought to check on Holly's whereabouts.

Smelling something burning, Russell asked, "What's that smell?"

"Oh, no - the cupcakes!" Joy cried. She ran over to open the oven, and was promptly greeted by the smell of smoke. She pulled the tray out to survey the damage.

"Are the cupcakes okay?" Dad asked.

"A little too done," Joy proposed, looking distraughtly at the tray of cupcakes in her hands.

Before they could figure out what to do, Abigail came through the door. Seeing the members of her family studying the tray of cupcakes, she knew it couldn't be good.

"What's up?" she asked.

They both turned to give her a blank stare, and Dad spoke first.

"The cupcakes are done," he offered.

Abigail sniffed the air and said, "I can tell. Maybe a little too done?"

She grabbed a cooling rack and dumped the pan of cupcakes onto it. Turning a few over, it was clear they were pretty black on the bottom.

"Looks like they are burned," she sighed, knowing they only

bought one cake mix, and that she was not interested in making another trip to the store.

Robby decided he had to do something to get their attention, so he magnified the sound of the blow drier.

"What's that humming noise?" Abigail asked.

The three of them paused to listen, and then looked curiously at each other.

"It's coming from the bathroom," Russell stated the obvious.

All three hurried to the bathroom, and Mom almost screamed when she saw Holly sitting in the bathtub with the blow dryer in her hand.

"Don't move, sweetie," she said cautiously, heading quickly over to unplug the hair dryer.

"Holly, what were you thinking?" Joy asked, while Russell rushed to get a towel and remove her from the tub.

"I wanted to look nice for the cookout," Holly said cheerfully.

"But you never blow dry your hair while you're sitting in water," Abigail explained to her youngest child. "You could have been electrocuted."

"Is that bad?" Holly asked innocently.

Russell, Abigail, and Joy all raised their eyebrows and looked at each other. Then drying Holly off, Mom simply replied, "Very bad."

She helped Holly get dressed while Joy returned to the kitchen to try to salvage any of the cupcakes. Wanting to get out of the bathroom and away from the blow dryer, Abigail said, "Come see what happened to the cupcakes."

Holly walked past her father and headed out the bathroom door to go check her cupcakes. As Mom walked past him, she said, "I'm throwing that blow dryer in the rubbish."

"Good idea," Dad agreed. "Just don't tell Joy. I think it belongs to her."

"Not any more," Mom whispered back. "As of today, it belongs to the dumpster."

Robby flew over and dropped onto the couch beside Daniel.

"That was a close one," he sighed, letting his head drop onto the back of the couch.

"Actually, a bit of an emotional roller coaster ride," Daniel offered.

Robby picked up his head and turned to give Daniel a bewildered look.

Seeing him waiting for an explanation, Daniel said, "I was laughing at Abigail vacuuming the driveway, and you were freaking out trying to figure out how to keep Holly from electrocuting herself."

Robby formed a silent "Oh" with his mouth and paused to visualize it all in his mind. Picturing Abigail with her vacuum out in the driveway, he asked, "Did it look really funny?"

Daniel smiled and said, "Oh, yeah, it was quite comical. I can't say I've ever seen anyone vacuuming their driveway before."

"Too bad Gabe missed all the excitement," Robby commented.

"Yeah, he's probably bouncing around out in the forest somewhere," Daniel commented, "trying to keep two boys from ramming their machines into a tree."

The two angels paused to listen to the conversation coming from the kitchen. Abigail had shown Holly how the cupcakes were all burned on the bottom. She reminded her that they had only bought one cake mix, so she didn't know what to do about it now. Yet Holly, always the optimist, quickly came up with a solution.

"It's okay, Mommy," she said, trying to make her feel better. "We'll just tell everyone they are chocolate on the bottom!"

Robby and Daniel chuckled at her solution.

"I don't care if they are burned on the bottom," Robby said, looking over at his fellow angel. "I would give anything to be able to sink my teeth into one of them right about now!"

****

The entire family gathered for a cook-out that night at dinnertime. Mom and Holly had worked hard frosting their "chocolate-bottomed" cupcakes, and had then made a fruit salad to go with the burgers.

104

Abigail couldn't have asked for a better family event. For a change, Joy was pleasant and didn't have any sarcastic comments. Maybe she decided that was a birthday gift for her mother. Whatever the case, Abigail deeply appreciated it. She missed those days of having her fun-loving daughter participating in family events.

Corey took a break from his ATV and roaming with Ryan, and even Holly was amusing and entertaining. No nagging or whining tonight, and she hadn't even spilled anything yet. She was very excited about the fruit salad she had helped make, and had a hard time waiting for dessert so she could serve her cupcakes.

Abigail looked around the picnic table and realized what a wonderful family she had. Seeing her husband at the other end of the table watching her, she paused to return his gaze and gave him a smile. They had known each other long enough to know what the look meant. They were both feeling extremely blessed.

What they didn't realize was that there were three more members of the family hanging out with them, silent and invisible, but still very present. Daniel, Gabriel, and Robert were hovering around the family barbeque observing the jovial interactions between the members of the Carter family. They couldn't help but smile as they did.

Looking at the food, Robby could stand no more. He let out with an almost audible groan and said, "What bothers me the most about being an angel in this family is seeing all this good food and not being able to eat any of it!"

Gabe chuckled and said, "I definitely agree with that. It looks like Abigail knows how to make a good burger, but I can't say for sure."

The three angels were almost salivating with their desire to dive into a burger and some salad. Knowing how useless it was to pine over something they couldn't have, Daniel decided to focus more on the family exchanges.

"Look at this family," he commented. "If this keeps up, we won't be needed much longer. They seem to have it all together right now."

"It does seem that way," Gabriel agreed.

"Aw, but will it last?" Robby asked.

He turned to face his cohorts. Neither of them had an answer for him. How would they know when their mission was finished? That wasn't a question they had asked before leaving the boundaries of Heaven. Surely the Father would somehow let them know when they had accomplished their task.

Plus, Robby had a good point. Would this family joviality last? Or was this just the calm before the storm? There was no way of knowing the answer to any of their questions. This was their first mission, and it was a new experience for all of them.

Just then Abigail got up from the table and headed for the house. She returned a few moments later with the tray filled with the cupcakes Holly had helped bake and decorate.

"Yeah, cupcakes!" Holly said excitedly. This was the moment she had been waiting for.

Holly would not let the family touch the cupcakes without first singing "Happy Birthday" to Mom. Once the singing was finished, Abigail had an announcement.

Holding up a cupcake, she said, "There is something I need to tell you before you take one of these cupcakes."

She turned the cupcake over to show the dark coloring on the bottom and explained, "Holly wanted you to know these are 'chocolate-bottomed' cupcakes."

Looking around the table, she saw a mixture of expressions. Corey and Russell each had a curious look on their face. Joy seemed more like she was trying hard to suppress a desire to laugh, while Holly was covering her mouth and having an extremely difficult time holding the giggles back.

Mom held up a butter knife and continued. "For those of you who don't believe that, here is a knife to cut the 'chocolate' off!"

The angels chuckled at Abigail's humor.

"I don't care if they are burned on the bottom," Robby smiled at his partners, "I would still give anything to take a huge bite out of one of those babies!"

Daniel and Gabriel could only nod their heads in agreement.

<+><+><+>

CHAPTER 10
AN ALMOST PERFECT DAY

Russell awoke with high hopes for the day. This was Abigail's birthday, and he was going to do all he could to give her the best day ever. He knew life had been challenging for her recently. Joy's attitude had been exasperating at times, and her behavior had been far from faultless. Corey was a restless boy, with sometimes destructive consequences. Then there was Holly's hyperactivity, which was something they could both use a break from.

Yes, he felt Abigail would greatly benefit with a day away from home. It would be fun for the two of them to spend quality time together, and not have to wonder what their trio of trouble was up to. What his three beautiful, restless, sometimes obnoxious children did today would be someone else's problem. Today, he and his lovely wife would be resting comfortably on the beach, soaking up the sun, and pretending they didn't have a care in the world.

He glanced out the window, and smiled with satisfaction. The sun was already shining, and it was a clear, blue sky. The weather couldn't have been any better if he had ordered it himself.

Yes, he smiled to himself, *this is going to be a great day!*

He climbed out of bed to check on the status of his troublesome trio. He wanted to make sure they were up and ready to shower their mother with love and affection as they served her with breakfast in bed.

Heading into the kitchen, he wasn't surprised to find Holly already at work. She was always so anxious to be involved, striving to bring joy and happiness into the lives of those around her.

"Good morning, sweetie," he said, giving her a quick hug.

"Morning, Daddy," she replied, as she dragged a chair over to the counter.

Reaching up to grab the toaster, she pulled it across the counter where she could reach it a little easier.

"Okay, let's talk about our plans, Daddy," she suggested.

"That sounds good," Russell agreed. "Who is doing what?"

"I will make the toast," she announced. "You can make an

egg for Mommy." Turning to look at her father, she added, "She likes them fried, you know."

Russell smiled at the seriousness on her face. She returned his smile, and then added, "and Corey will make the coffee."

"Sounds like you remembered the plan," he smiled at his youngest daughter's summary of events.

Just then, Corey joined them in the kitchen. Overhearing Holly's run down of the plans, he said, "You might need to help me with the coffee, Dad. It isn't my specialty."

"Sure, just let me get the egg started," Russell said, opening the refrigerator door.

Russell went to work on the egg preparation, Holly popped some bread into the toaster, and then they focused on getting the coffeemaker set up. The coffeemaker was being less than cooperative, and the three members of the Carter family soon forgot about the eggs and the toast while the process of making coffee swallowed up their attention.

Almost simultaneously, the group noticed the smell of burned toast.

"Oh, no, my toast!" Holly cried in alarm.

Dad suddenly remembered his egg cooking in the frying pan, and realized it hadn't faired any better than the toast.

Joy chose exactly that moment to breeze into the kitchen. "Smells like you guys are doing a great job with Mom's breakfast," she said scornfully.

Her comment was emotionally painful to those who were trying hard to give their mother a special treat. Corey was not one to fight back, but he didn't appreciate his sister's sarcasm or lack of family involvement in this event.

"Oh, yeah, Joy," he shot back at her. "Do you think you can do any better?!"

She smiled snidely at him and said, "Well, at least I don't burn toast."

Corey had always remained a silent party to Joy's teenage attitude. Her spiteful remarks had been bothering him for a long time, but he had always chosen to walk away and ignore them. She was his older sister, and he had always respected that. Not today, though. Today was different. They were trying to do something special for Mom, and not only was she choosing not to participate, but she was bold enough to criticize their efforts in the process. He was tired of the strain her attitude was putting on their family, and now was as good a time as any to let her know.

"What do you do around here?" he demanded, and then added, "Other than think about yourself all the time? 'Cause it doesn't look like you're doing anything to make Mom's birthday special."

Watching for a reaction from Joy, he was disappointed when she didn't bother to respond, or even attempt to make eye contact with him.

"Life isn't all about you, Joy!" he yelled across the kitchen at her.

Russell was about to step into the argument between his two teenage children, but stopped a moment to consider the direction of the conversation. What Corey had said was all true, and maybe it would be beneficial for Joy to hear it from someone other than her parents, for a change.

Joy's next action caught him by surprise. He had expected her to come back with some cynical comment and then stomp dramatically out of the room. That had become her trademark in recent months. Instead, Joy headed to the refrigerator as if she was on a mission. She pulled the door open, dragged out the bowl of fruit salad left over from the barbeque the previous night, and took a plate from the cupboard. Grabbing a serving utensil, she slapped a spoonful of fruit salad onto the plate. Then she turned to address the three individuals staring at her.

"There!" she stated triumphantly, "I just contributed some fruit salad to Mom's breakfast in bed!"

With that, she turned and waltzed out of the kitchen, making the dramatic exit that Russell had expected earlier.

Corey turned to look at his father, wondering what he thought about the whole transaction. Russell gave his son a quick smile, shook his head and said, "Well, I guess we better start over with the egg and the toast."

From the comfort of her bedroom, Abigail let out a groan and covered her head with a pillow. Listening to her family arguing and burning breakfast in the kitchen was a painful experience. It would almost be better if she just got up and made her own breakfast, but she knew her family was doing their best to give her a special treat. So, as difficult as it might be to stay in bed and listen to it all, she would do it. She just hoped Joy's behavior didn't spoil everything, and prayed that the rest of the family wouldn't catch the kitchen on fire.

****

After finding success in their second attempt at making a fried egg and toast, Russell, Corey, and Holly jubilantly marched into the bedroom to serve their favorite family member her special birthday breakfast. On the way in, they had invited Joy to join them, but as expected, she had turned down the offer.

Holly climbed into the middle of the bed and chatted freely while her mother ate. Russell and Corey sat on the edge and joined in the conversation as often as Holly allowed. The day may have had a faulty start, but it seemed to have gained momentum and was going well at the moment.

While the family dined with Mom in the bedroom, the angels relaxed in the living room. Daniel was stretched out on the couch, Gabriel at ease in Russell's recliner, and Robby was stretched out across the floor, lying on his side.

"Your man, Corey, sure let Joy have a piece of his mind," Robby commented to Gabriel.

Gabriel nodded in agreement and said, "I noticed. It's unusual for him to speak his mind, so she must have really struck a nerve."

"Well, maybe it will do some good," Robby suggested.

"I hope so," Daniel spoke up, "but I worry that it might have some repercussions. Joy is a bit unpredictable."

The three angels stopped to contemplate it, realizing that Daniel did have a point. It hadn't been as easy to redirect her as they had thought it would be. She did seem to be very self-absorbed and determined to have her own way. Comments from family members that were intended as advice or guidance were usually perceived as criticism and invasive. Nothing seemed to reach into her realm of selfishness to make her want to improve her attitude.

During their moments of reflection, the harmonious voices of four of the five-member Carter family could be heard coming from the bedroom.

"Well, at least most of the family is happy," Robby commented.

Daniel smiled when he heard Holly laugh, and said, "That much is true. I just wish Joy would realize what she is missing with her narcissistic attitude."

"At least she didn't storm out the door when Corey confronted her," Gabriel surmised.

"True," Daniel said, ponderingly, "but I don't know if we are making progress yet or not. The fact that she didn't rush out and chose to retreat quietly to her room does not necessarily mean anything."

He turned to look at his friends and said, "This may just be the calm before the storm. I don't know what it will take to get through to her and make her want to change her ways."

Robby and Gabriel returned his gaze, but couldn't give him words of reassurance. She was unfamiliar territory to all of them. None of them had ever raised a teenage daughter. They would do their best to continue to reach her, but were beginning to question if they had the skills it would take.

****

Once Mom was finished with her breakfast in bed, she headed out to clean the kitchen. Holly offered to do it for her, but Abigail insisted Holly had done her job in preparing the meal, so Mom would do the clean up. She told Holly to go pick out some books and toys that she could bring to Aunt Carrie's house before they had to leave.

Russell followed her out to the kitchen and, as they washed

the dishes, he talked about plans for the day. He was anxious to head to the beach for a quiet day of relaxation.

"I don't want to miss church and really should stay home and do some laundry," Abigail told him.

Russell turned to face his wife and asked, "Seriously, Abigail? You would rather go to church and do laundry instead of going to the beach for the day with no kids?"

Abigail smiled at her husband. Church had been beneficial to her and she hated to miss it, plus she also knew how far behind she was on laundry. If Joy didn't have any clean underwear for school, she would freak out. Yet, a day at the beach with no kids was a very tempting offer.

"What kind of a question is that?" she finally responded. "Of course I would rather go to the beach, but who is going to do the laundry?"

Russell walked over and gave his wife a hug. "I'll tell you what – when we get home, I'll help you with the laundry." Pausing for a moment, he added, "And I'm sure the world won't end if you miss one day of church."

"I suppose," Abigail said, returning his hug. "But you better keep your end of the deal. The laundry doesn't go away on its own, you know."

Russell smiled, kissed his wife on the forehead, and vowed he would be true to his word.

Abigail picked up a dish cloth and walked over to wash the table just as Joy came walking into the kitchen. She carried her purse and appeared to be heading out.

"Where are you going?" Russell casually asked her.

She stopped and turned to face her father, looking at him almost with disbelief written on her face.

"Do I ask you where you are going every time you leave the house?" she demanded.

"Am I your child?" Russell retorted smartly. "You, young lady, are still my child and my responsibility, so that means I have the right to know where you are going."

"I just get tired of you nagging me all the time," Joy yelled, stomping off toward the front door.

"You didn't tell me where you are going yet," Russell was not about to let her get away without answering his question. It was a legitimate question, and as her father, he wasn't being unreasonable to ask it.

"To go pick Amber up and bring her back for the day," Joy threw her purse over her shoulder and left, slamming the door behind her.

Russell didn't want to put a damper on Abigail's special day, but his daughter's behavior was unacceptable. He hurried over to the door and opened it to call out to her.

"Don't burn all your bridges, Harmonie Lane," he called after her. "With that kind of an attitude, you might find yourself on an isolated island with no access to the mainland!"

Joy didn't respond. She hopped into her car and flew off out of the yard. Whether she had heard him or not wasn't clear, but Russell felt bad for yelling and adding another flaw to their less than perfect morning. He turned back into the kitchen to apologize to his wife.

"Sorry about that, honey," he started, "I just wish every once in awhile I could have a normal conversation with her – one that doesn't always end up in an argument."

However, he was surprised to see a smile on his wife's face. She was still washing the table, but didn't seem to be perturbed over the spat between father and daughter. Instead, she surprised him with her comment.

"That was pretty good, Russell," she complimented him. Seeing his inquisitive expression, she added, "That thing about burning your bridges and being on an isolated island. Did you come up with that on your own, or was that something your mother used to say?"

Russell smirked at her humor and said, "To be honest, I'm not really sure. It might have been something my mother used to say, but that would have been a long time ago."

He paused to think about it, then looking at his wife he chuckled and said, "That was pretty good, though, wasn't it?! Sometimes, I wish she did live on an island!"

"Or we did," Abigail suggested. "There are days I wish I was alone on an island with no access to the mainland."

Russell smiled at his wife and said, "Well, I can't take you to an island today, but I promise I will at least get you to the beach – with no mouthy teenagers to deal with!"

Abigail looked around the kitchen and, satisfied that it was clean enough, she said, "Sounds good. I'll grab some beach towels and pack some snacks. You grab the beach chairs and umbrella, and I'll meet you in the driveway."

Anxious to get Abigail out of the house before she changed her mind, or anything else went wrong, Russell headed for the garage to find the beach chairs and umbrella. Calling back over his shoulder, he asked, "Can you grab my coconut oil, too? It's pretty sunny out here, and I don't want to get a sun burn."

Having watched Joy heading for her car and knowing the rest of the family would soon follow suit, the angels had decided to make some quick plans for the day.

"So, it looks like I am heading to Ryan's to chase the boys around today," Gabriel commented. "I wish I could convince them to play video games instead of riding ATVs. Anyone have any ideas?"

The other two angels smirked, and Daniel said, "I don't think there is much we can do about that. It's kind of out of our jurisdiction."

Robby patted Gabriel on the back and added, "You just gotta go with the flow, man." Thinking about the day ahead of him, he said, "I just hope I don't have another run in with the bear at Aunt Carrie's house."

Daniel raised his eyebrows and said, "Yeah, and I hope I can keep Joy and Amber out of trouble. Can you imagine what they might get into here in the house all alone with no adult supervision?"

"Sounds like a recipe for disaster," Gabriel sighed. After a moment of silence, he said, "I think we all better keep our bells handy. It sounds like any one of us could use some extra help at any moment."

"Very true," Daniel agreed. Then seeing the family climbing into the car, he added, "Good luck, guys, and ring if you need anything." Turning to fly off, he threw over his shoulder, "I better fly if I want to catch up with Joy!"

****

Russell and Abigail dropped Corey off at Ryan's house, and then headed to Aunt Carrie's to leave Holly. Once the kids had been deposited, they set their sites for the beach. Although it wasn't a long ride, they couldn't seem to get there fast enough. The thought of a full day of sun, sand, and relaxation was very motivating. No nagging, no demands, no sarcastic remarks coming from any ungrateful kids. Just adult conversation accompanied by peace and quiet. Both Russell and Abigail silently reasoned that with such a beautiful day ahead of them, what could possibly go wrong?

After parking the car, they found the perfect spot on the beach, and Russell pitched the umbrella while Abigail set out the beach chairs. Then they settled down to enjoy their quiet time. Abigail pulled out a book and Russell went to work coating himself with a layer of coconut oil.

As he spread out his beach towel, he said, "This wouldn't be any better if we were on a Caribbean vacation."

"I will agree with that," Abigail smiled from under her hat. "It may not be the Caribbean, but it is good enough for me. It has sun, sand, water and no kids. That sounds just about divine to me!"

Russell settled on his towel and sighed. "I can second that," he said. Turning to look up at his wife, he added, "Not that I don't love my children, but today, they are someone else's problem."

Abigail leaned against the back of her chair and closed her eyes dreamily. In response to her husband's comment, she said, "They will always be our problem, Russell, no matter who they might be staying with."

"Very true, my dear, very true," Russell agreed. "But enough talk about the kids. I'm just gonna soak up some sun and maybe even take a nap. How long did you want to stay today?"

Without opening her eyes or pausing to think about it, Abigail replied, "How about forever?!"

Russell chuckled and said, "Sounds good to me." Rolling over onto his stomach, he said, "Just let me know when forever is over and you're ready to do something else."

Naturally, their day of relaxation went quicker than either of them wanted it to. They had brought water and snacks with them, but decided before heading home, they would like to stop for a nice dinner at their favorite restaurant, The Seafood Alley. It had been quite some time since they had taken the time or money to enjoy a leisurely dinner there. Plus, a romantic candlelight dinner at their favorite restaurant would top off their perfect day at the beach.

Realizing they had stayed at the beach longer than they had intended, and knowing that they would return later than planned if they stopped for a dinner, Abigail decided she should make some phone calls. She first checked in with Aunt Carrie, who was quick to reassure her all was well and that she didn't mind at all if they were late getting home. Checking in with Ryan's parents produced the same results. Since there was no school the next day, they didn't mind if Corey hung out with them a little later either.

Abigail then called Joy to see how things were going at home. Joy was quick to reassure her that she and Amber had been having a good day. All was well, and of course, she didn't mind if her parents would be later than originally planned. Amber would stay and keep her company, and maybe they would check with her parents to see if she could spend the night.

With everything seemingly in order, Russell and Abigail began to pack up their beach accessories to head out for a fine dining experience at The Seafood Alley. Abigail's birthday had been nothing short of wonderful, and Russell was grateful everything had gone so well.

****

However, the sun had not set, and the day was not yet over. Shortly after Joy received the call from her parents about being late, Shane and Devin showed up at the Carter household.

"How did they know we were here?" Joy asked, clearly surprised as she watched them getting out of their car.

"I told them," Amber replied nonchalantly.

116

"But you knew my parents said we couldn't have any guests," Joy stated, trying to politely reprimand her best friend.

"Who's going to know?" Amber asked. "Your parents said they are going to be late anyway. They will never know they were even here."

Joy hoped that was true. Yet, she knew that parents somehow had a way of finding things out. This had been her first opportunity to prove herself, and if her parents found out the boys had come to visit, they would never let her have the house to herself again.

She soon found out that Shane and Devin were not interested in hanging out at her house, though. Hearing that Joy's parents wouldn't be home until quite a bit later, they presented their plans for the evening.

"Look at what we have," Devin announced, as he pulled his wallet from his back pocket.

He held up what appeared to be a couple of driver's licenses, and the girls came closer to inspect them. They were extremely surprised to see their photos on the cards.

"What are those?" Amber asked, not quite sure what was going on.

"Remember when we went to the mall and had our pictures taken in the photo booth?" Devin asked.

Joy and Amber both had puzzled looks on their faces and simply nodded their heads. Neither girl was sure what that had to do with the cards he now held in front of them.

"Yeah," Shane said with a drawl. "Devin had your pictures put on some fake IDs so we can go to the bar."

The two girls stared at each other with blank expressions. They had never been to a bar, and weren't sure they wanted to go now. However, Devin and Shane were quite convinced it was something the two couples should attempt.

"It will be great," Devin tried to reassure them. "We each have an ID to show we are of age, and I heard there is an awesome band playing tonight for the holiday weekend."

"Yeah," Shane agreed, "no school tomorrow and your parents won't be home for hours, so we have plenty of time to go hang out and listen to the music. Who will ever know? We'll be home before your parents get there."

Joy and Amber were in agreement that they would like to go listen to the band, but neither of them had ever done anything this risky before. They tried to come up with an argument as to why the plan wouldn't work, but Devin and Shane wouldn't hear of it. The plan sounded too perfect to them to let the opportunity slip away.

Finally Joy agreed, but stated they needed to be home long before her parents arrived. She would bring her cell phone and keep in touch with her parents so they would know when it was time to leave the bar. With the plans made, Joy and Amber hopped into the car with Devin and Shane and headed downtown to the local bar.

The foursome tried to act mature as they approached the door, not sure how convincing their fake IDs would be. They didn't have any trouble getting in, though, and found a quiet table in the corner where they could relax while listening to the band.

Daniel gave a groan when the group was allowed entrance to the joint. He had been hoping someone would recognize the IDs as counterfeits and send the two couples away. Now he would really have his hands full trying to keep the four of them out of trouble.

At first all seemed to be going well. They just seemed like a couple of kids out having fun, enjoying the music, while keeping to themselves. However, after Devin and Shane had a beer or two, they began to get obnoxious. Joy and Amber seemed reluctant to be seen with them, but knew they couldn't leave since they had all come together in the same car. So they decided to move over to the bar instead, thus putting some space between them.

Daniel hovered close to Joy, wanting to do all in his power to keep her safe. What he really wanted was to get her out of there, but he wasn't sure how to accomplish that feat. As he was pondering some potential escape plans, he noticed a coarse looking man watching Joy intently. He was a big, burly looking man, and not one that Daniel would want to encounter alone on a dark night. Daniel only hoped that he kept his distance from Joy.

However, a few minutes later Daniel's fears materialized

when the husky, unkempt man moved over to a bar stool closer to Joy.

"Hi, there, beautiful," he said smoothly as he sat down on the stool. "My name is Bill. What's yours?"

Joy glanced over at him and hesitated. She didn't want to strike up a conversation with a stranger, and he didn't seem to be her type anyway. Yet, on the other hand, she didn't want to be rude. So she simply replied, "Harmonie," choosing to use her legal name.

"Huh, that's different," Bill said into his glass of beer.

Daniel had done well staying in the background and not revealing himself, but he felt he needed to take on some earthly features if he was going to be able to protect Joy in this situation. So he slipped into the corner, where no one would notice his sudden appearance, and then walked out hoping he could be Joy's knight in shining armor.

At first, he felt very awkward. He was not accustomed to hanging out in a bar. As a drug and alcohol counselor during his lifetime, it had not been a part of his nature to acquaint himself with establishments that sold alcoholic beverages. He didn't really care to be here now, but he had one very unruly teenager that he needed to protect and try to rescue.

Knowing that "Burly Bill" was trying to strike up a conversation with Joy and Amber, he decided he had better not waste any time in heading their direction. The girls didn't seem to be too interested in what Bill was saying, but that didn't seem to deter him. He just kept leaning their way and attempting to engage them in a conversation.

Daniel strolled over and bravely sat on the bar stool located directly between Joy and Burly Bill.

"Is this seat taken?" he asked, glancing over at Joy.

She turned and gave him a startled look. Her gaze lingered for a moment, before she replied that it was not occupied. He wasn't sure if it was his sudden appearance that had startled her, or if she recognized him from the night when he had posed as a police officer and tried to keep her from walking across town alone. Fortunately, she said nothing and returned to her conversation with

Amber, dismissing Daniel as though he didn't even exist.

He sat at the bar, feeling about as uneasy as he had ever felt in his lifetime, and quite unsure of what he should do now that he had made his presence known. Burly Bill had an idea of his own, though.

"Why don't you find someplace else to sit?" he suggested. "I was having a conversation with these young ladies."

Daniel had chosen that seat for a reason, and he was not about to give it up. Now that he had a physical body, he intended to keep it strategically placed between the subject he was protecting on his right and the burly, obnoxious man on the left - until he could figure out how to get Joy out of there, anyway.

"This seat is fine, thank you," Daniel tried to be polite. Turning to face Joy, he said, "We shouldn't be here, Joy."

Joy turned sharply to face him. "How did you know my name?" she demanded.

"He doesn't," Burly Bill commented, "cause your name is Harmonie."

Daniel glanced briefly at him, and then had to think fast to explain how he would happen to know Joy's name. "I heard the boys you came in with talking to you," he quickly explained.

The answer apparently satisfied Joy, but she still had her guard up and wasn't sure if Daniel was a friend or foe.

Trying again, Daniel gingerly approached the subject of leaving. "Don't you think you should go home now?" he asked.

Joy turned to look at Daniel in exasperation and said, "What business is that of yours? I am here with friends, and I will go home when I am ready!" She paused, and then defiantly added, "And I am not ready yet."

Daniel rubbed the palm of his hand across his chin, wondering what he could do to convince Joy to go home. The sooner he got her out of there and back into the safety of the Carter household, the better he would feel. Right now, they were walking on thin ice, and he had never been one who liked to take risks. However, before he could come up with another idea, Burly Bill stepped back into the picture.

"Why don't you leave her alone?" he asked, looking sideways

at Daniel. "What are you to her anyway, her guardian angel?"

He smirked at his humor, but Daniel's face colored a bit, realizing that is exactly what he was to Joy. He knew he wasn't supposed to reveal his identity to her, but he was desperate. He wanted Joy out of this bar, and he wanted her out now.

Looking at Bill, he asked, "And what if I am? Maybe I am her guardian angel."

If Burly Bill had smirked before, this time he outright laughed. "Sure you are, mister," he chuckled. "And I'm the president of the United States."

Daniel ignored his sarcasm, and focused his attention on Joy. Leaning around to look her in the face, he said, "Come on, Joy. My mission is to keep you safe, so let me just take you home. You shouldn't be here."

Joy had had enough of Daniel's persistence. She looked him squarely in the eyes and said, "Would you just leave me alone? I don't know who you are, and I'm not going anywhere with you."

Burly Bill was quick to come to Joy's defense. "Listen, mister," he said, "I have spent a lot of time sitting at this bar, and you are the first one who has ever tried to get a pretty lady to go home with him by claiming to be her guardian angel."

He paused to wait for Daniel's reaction, but when there wasn't one, he continued, "So where are your wings, angel?"

Daniel still didn't react, so Burly Bill pushed it a little further. He stood up and started flapping his arms, pretending he had wings of his own.

"Come on, Angel Man," he taunted, "show me how you fly. If you're an angel, you must be able to fly."

It was a very intimidating situation for Daniel, but he tried to ignore the insult and concentrate on his mission to get Joy out of there. When Daniel failed to react, Burly Bill dropped back down onto his bar stool. Joy and Amber were trying hard to ignore both of the men located next to them, as well as the interactions between the two. Yet, neither of them had moved away from their placement at the bar.

Starting to feel a little anxious and distraught over the involvement of the hefty man beside him, Daniel stood up and said,

"Let's go, Joy. It's time to go home. This is just not the place for you."

His actions brought Burly Bill to his feet as well. "She's not going anywhere, buddy," he announced. "If she wants to stay here, that's her choice. And if you try to take her out of here, you're going to have to get her past me." With that, he placed himself strategically between Joy and the exit.

Daniel knew he was in trouble and reached for his silver bell. It was time to call for back up. He wasn't sure where Gabe and Robby were, but it couldn't be as important as the situation he was in.

Fortunately, both angels arrived almost instantly. Daniel saw them before anyone else, since they appeared first in their angelic form, being invisible to the human eye. It didn't take them long to sum up the situation and take on a human appearance. If Daniel was in manifested form, there must be a good reason for it.

Gabriel and Robby slowly moved closer to Daniel. They wanted to be close enough to hear the conversation, but not move so fast as to draw attention to themselves. As they got within an audible range, they could hear the big, husky brute arguing with Daniel.

"Just back off, bud," he was saying. "This girl is fine. She's a big girl and, she can take care of herself. She doesn't need any 'guardian angels' looking out for her."

Daniel looked past him at Gabe and Robby and raised an eyebrow. If Burly Bill thought Joy didn't need a guardian angel, then he didn't know Joy.

"Look, mister," Daniel pleaded with him, "I'm not trying to cause any problems here. I just want to take Joy home."

"And I said she's not going," Bill insisted.

Suddenly a crowd seemed to form around them. Burly Bill's loud, obnoxious comments must have drawn the attention of the patrons around them. Sensing that a fight was about to ensue, the other occupants of the bar formed a circle. Shane and Devin broke through the circle and asked what was happening. Before Daniel could attempt to explain the situation, not that he could explain it in a way that would make sense anyway, everything fell apart. It was probably as simple as an unintentional push or a misguided arm movement, but obnoxious Burly Bill felt threatened. In his intoxicated state, he mistook whatever the movement was for an act of aggression, and the whole bar room seemed to explode with activity, and not in a pleasant way either.

Patrons who minutes before had been oblivious to the argument between Daniel and Burly Bill, now, for some reason, felt it was their responsibility to get involved and throw a few punches of their own. Fists met faces or guts, and beer bottles flew through the air. The angels were caught off guard, and didn't know how to react. This was not a situation Daniel or Gabriel had ever been in before. Robert, having maintained a livelier lifestyle, was a little more in his element. At first, he only stood there and chuckled, but when Daniel and Gabe gave him an unappreciative look, he quickly sobered up.

Joy and Amber found a corner to huddle in, but still seemed reluctant to leave. Maybe it was because they couldn't go without Shane and Devin, and the two boys were right in the middle of the action. Or, maybe they were concerned for their safety and didn't want to leave until they knew they could get safely out the door. Whatever their reason for staying, the angels didn't have a chance to remove them from the bar before they heard sirens and saw police entering the room.

"Uh-oh," said Robby, seeing the men in uniform running through the door.

The police wasted no time in breaking up the fight. They separated the brawling men and put distance between them. Then they started handcuffing drunken patrons and carting them off to the police station one-by-one. Daniel watched in horror as Joy and Amber were taken off with the rest of them.

With all the activity of the past few moments, the angels forgot about their earthly appearance. One of the officers headed their way and said, "What about these guys? Were they involved in this brawl?"

"Oh, no, officer," Daniel was quick to defend himself. "We weren't doing anything wrong."

"That's right," Robby agreed. "We are just a couple of angels trying to come to the rescue of a couple of innocent girls."

The officer looked at the trio and gave a derisive snort. "Sure you are," he smiled sarcastically at them. "We find lots of angels hanging out at the bar trying to help girls out."

He looked across the bar room at his partner and called, "Hey, John, do you have any room in your car for these three 'angels'?"

What the officer did not realize was that as soon as he turned his back, the angels had used the opportunity to resume their angelic appearance. They instantly disappeared from human sight.

His partner looked across the room at him and called back, "What angels?"

Pointing over his shoulder, he said, "These guys right here...." His voice trailed off as he turned and failed to focus on anything but open space. "What the heck? They were here just a second ago."

****

Russell and Abigail had just finished a wonderful candlelight dinner at The Seafood Alley Restaurant and were cherishing their last moments of freedom before heading home. Neither one of them could believe what a perfect day they had just had. The weather had been absolutely divine, and they had enjoyed every minute on the beach. Now they had topped it off with a marvelous meal that couldn't have been any better. They had forgotten life could be this good. Just then Abigail's cell phone rang.

"Mom, I need some help," Joy's distressed voice came through the phone. Abigail couldn't tell if she was crying, or if was just a bad connection.

"What's the matter, honey?" she asked her eldest daughter.

"I'm at the police station, and I need you to come get me," Joy reluctantly told her mother.

Abigail grew serious and gave Russell a panicked look. Remembering Joy's need to get her front wheel fixed, Abigail became concerned. "What happened? Did you have a car accident?"

"No, it wasn't an accident," Joy said sadly. "I'll explain when you get here. Just come as soon as you can."

"We are just finishing up with dinner at the beach. Where are you?" Abigail questioned.

"I'm at Franklin County," Joy replied.

"Okay, we'll be there as soon as we can," Mom reassured her daughter.

When she finished their conversation, she told Russell that they needed to go get Joy at the police station. She didn't have a lot of details, but they needed to get there as soon as they could. Russell told his wife that they would need to go home so he could shower first.

"Your daughter is in distress at the police station, and you want to shower first?" she asked incredulously.

"I reek of coconut oil," he explained to his wife. "I can't go rescue my daughter smelling like I just came back from the Bahamas!"

"Okay," Abigail agreed, "but we need to hurry."

They drove as fast as they dared, all the while growing anxious about whatever kind of dilemma Joy might have found her way into this time. When they got home, Russell hurried to the bedroom to find a change of clothing. Abigail restlessly paced the kitchen. What could have possibly gone wrong? Joy said it wasn't an accident, but what other reason could there be for her to need rescuing from the police station?

Abigail could hear Russell muttering in the bedroom, opening and closing bureau drawers. Finally, he called out to her.

"Hey, Abigail, where are my clean underwear?" he cried out in frustration.

Abigail groaned, remembering their conversation from this morning.

"I told you I needed to do some laundry!" she called back. "But you wanted to go to the beach. So go without, or put the coconut scented ones back on!"

Russell rushed past her, heading to the bathroom to take a brief shower.

"I know, it's my fault," he admitted. "I told you I would help you with the laundry when we got home. I'll just put the coconut scented ones back on, and then coat myself with a layer of cologne!"

As anxious as Abigail was right now, she gave a derisive little snort and said a silent prayer of thanks for the invention of cologne.

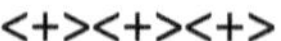

CHAPTER 11
TROUBLED TRIOS

It was a silent ride home from the Franklin County Police Station. A troubled trio sat uncomfortably in the Carter family car. It wasn't the normal trio of trouble, though. Usually the trio was comprised of the Carter children. Tonight's trio included Joy, as usual, but also integrated Abigail and Russell. The trip home tonight was a painful process for all three of them.

Even though it was surprisingly quiet in the car, it didn't necessarily mean that they were in a peaceful state of mind. Far from it was more likely the case. The battles that raged within each individual were comparable to a full, robust war.

Russell was internally beating up on himself. He wondered where he had failed as a father figure. He had tried to be firm, yet also remain loving. He had always been an active part of the family life in his household, and had worked hard to be nurturing, while still providing clear guidelines for his children. Where had he gone wrong? Had he been too lenient with Joy somewhere along the way? He wasn't known to drink or hang out at a bar. What had made her decide to go to the bar on her first opportunity to experience a little pre-adult freedom? He had given her a chance to prove herself, and instead she had repaid him with a slap in the face.

Abigail was thinking back through all the fun, family times they had spent together, and wondered why that hadn't been enough for Joy. As mother of the family, she had always been the family planner. She had kept the kids active and busy, searching the newspapers continuously to find quality activities that they could do together. Yet, lately, it was like Joy had built a wall around herself and wanted to be isolated from her family. How could it have come to this? Was Joy ashamed of her family? Were they not exciting enough for her? Were they an embarrassment to her? Why didn't spending time with her family mean anything to her anymore?

Joy sat silently in the back seat, and the internal battle raging within her was due to the agony of not knowing what her parents were thinking. It was nothing short of excruciating for her to sit there in silence. She had expected a scolding, some reprimanding, yelling or screaming – anything but the silence that surrounded her. What were they thinking? Why weren't they saying anything? What was going to happen when they got home? Would she be grounded until the day she moved out?

Finally, Joy could no longer take it. She called out, "Would someone please just say something?!"

"What do you want us to say, Joy?" her father asked.

"I don't know," Joy replied in exasperation. "Just say something, anything, because the silent treatment is killing me!"

Mom looked briefly over her shoulder, sighed and said, "What point is there in trying to talk to you, Joy? You haven't listened to anything we have said for a long time now, so why waste our breath. Words just don't seem to matter to you anymore."

"How about if I say I'm sorry," Joy suggested. "Would those words make a difference?"

"Do you think that would really help?" Dad asked. "Like saying you're sorry will make everything okay?"

"If it means anything to you," Joy began, "I didn't think it would come to this. We just wanted to go listen to the music."

"It didn't bother you to go to a bar, as a minor, using a fake ID?" Mom questioned. "A place where you knew you were not old enough to be, and in a room full of adults drinking alcohol, which you're not allowed to drink?"

"Okay, so it was a bad idea," Joy agreed.

"It wasn't a bad idea," Dad spoke up.

Joy looked up with surprise, and saw him looking at her in the mirror.

"It was a terrible idea," he completed his thought.

Joy sighed and racked her brain trying to find something to say to ease the tension between the three of them. The trio sat in silence for a few minutes more, and then it was Mom who spoke up.

"You know, Joy," she started, "we have put our heart and soul into raising you correctly. We have taught you the value of spending time together as a family. Do you remember what your father said this morning about burning bridges?"

Joy thought back to this morning, which seemed so long ago. What was it that her father had said? Oh, yeah, he had said something about burning bridges and finding yourself alone on an isolated island. Did that mean her parents were giving up on her?

"You would turn your back on your own child?" Joy asked incredulously.

"Patience has a limit," Mom explained, sounding defeated. "We can only take so much, and you have been a challenge for quite some time now."

Russell joined the conversation and said, "And don't forget that there are two other children in this family. We can't let them slip through the cracks while we focus all our attention on you."

"Did you know we had to ditch them on your Aunt Carrie and Ryan's parents tonight?" Abigail asked her daughter.

Joy had been so wrapped up in herself, as she had been for much of the past year or so, that she hadn't thought about her siblings. Yet, she still wasn't ready to go down without a fight.

"So, what you are saying is that I'm more work than I am worth?" she demanded from her parents.

"That's not what we are saying at all," Dad said in total frustration.

Mom looked over her shoulder at her eldest daughter, the child she had loved since the day she was born, and asked, "What do you want from us, Joy? We have done all we can since the moment we first laid eyes on you to give you the best childhood possible. We tried to keep you happy, healthy, and safe. You were never deprived or abused. We have taken you places and tried to show you how wonderful family life can be. We never neglected your needs. We have always been here for you."

She paused and looked away before continuing. "But in the last year or so, you have acted like you didn't want to be seen with us, or even have anything to do with your family. You've been sarcastic and rude, and take everything we say to you as criticism. I just don't know what to say or do to make you happy anymore."

Russell listened to his wife's patient explanation, and he

wanted to cheer out loud. He thought his comment about burning bridges was good, but she was doing an excellent job at scoring some home runs herself. She sounded like an experienced counselor, like one who had been working with teenagers all her life. Where had she acquired such knowledge?

Joy was doing some thinking of her own. She was feeling a bit guilty and quite defeated as well. She wanted to defend herself, but she knew her parents were right. She hadn't treated them well lately, and she had no excuses to offer for her behavior. She just wanted to be an adult and on her own. As an adult, she wouldn't need someone correcting her all the time, or pointing out things she should do differently. Yet, the fact remained that as much as she wanted it, she was not quite an adult yet, and that was not her parents' fault. However, she had been treating them like it was.

When she couldn't find words to suffice, she finally offered a quiet plea. "I don't know what to say, Mom," was all she could come up with.

Abigail was pleased that Joy was not arguing, and hopeful that maybe something they were saying was finally getting through to her.

"Then let's not say anything right now," she suggested. "It's better to say nothing than to get upset and say things we don't mean."

"That sounds like a good plan," Dad agreed. "We'll sleep on it tonight, and then deal with it in the morning when the three of us aren't so upset."

With the trio in agreement, for the first time in a long time, the rest of the ride home was done in a silent atmosphere. Although the words were not openly voiced, all three of them still had many unspoken thoughts rolling around in their heads.

****

Following along behind the Carter car was another troubled trio. They had opted to trail along behind the car, instead of riding in it. For one thing, they weren't sure they wanted to hear the battle that might be raging inside. The other reason was that they had plenty to talk about between themselves. They flew along at the rear of the car, keeping within adequate distance to make sure the family was safe, but allowing them the privacy of dealing with Joy's behavior on their own.

"How could we have let it come to this?" Daniel said, beating up on himself. "I should have stepped in sooner."

"But how could we have known what would happen?" Gabriel counter argued. "We weren't given the ability to see into the future. We had no way of knowing she would end up at the jail."

Looking at the car ahead of them, Robby questioned, "I wonder what's going on in there."

By choosing to remain on the exterior side of the car, they hadn't heard the words of wisdom her parents had shared with Joy. From their position outside, they couldn't tell if there was a battle raging in the interior or if Joy was in tears of repentance. Knowing Joy, though, they were almost sure it wasn't the latter.

The car pulled into the Carter homestead, and the troubled trio from inside quietly exited the car and walked into the house. Seeing the sagging of Russell and Abigail's shoulders broke the angels' hearts. They felt as if they had failed their mission here on Earth. Within moments, there was an angelic trio having a battle themselves.

"What have we done?" Robby asked sorrowfully.

"I think it's more like 'What have we not done?'" Daniel suggested. "We failed to keep Joy out of trouble."

"And where do we stand?" Gabriel questioned. "If Heaven finds out we were hanging out in a bar and almost got arrested, we could lose our wings."

"And I was lucky the first time I got them," Robby stated. "If I lose my wings from this mission, I will never get them back again."

Daniel and Gabriel looked quizzically at him. It did seem selfish to be thinking about their own needs when the Carter family was in such a state, but on the other hand, it was a good point. They all stood the risk of losing out tonight.

"We should have never taken this assignment," Robby said

in frustration, realizing that not only was it more challenging than they had expected, but they also ran the risk of failing.

Turning his head a bit and giving him a sideways look, Gabriel asked, "But how did we know it would come to this? Joy has been unpredictable right from the start."

Daniel knew that Joy had been a challenge, but she wasn't the only Carter child that had been difficult. As frustrated as he was, he suddenly felt the need to defend her.

"Oh, and you think Corey is an angel?" he asked Gabe.

Gabriel was taken by surprise, not expecting Daniel to attack his subject. "I didn't say he was perfect. He has his faults, but at least he didn't end up at the police station tonight in handcuffs!"

"But she didn't really do anything worthy of getting arrested," Daniel continued his defense.

"Oh, so going to a bar with a fake ID, and pretending you're older than you are, while drinking beer with your friends is acceptable behavior from a minor?" Gabe shot back at him.

"Yeah," Robby agreed with him, "no one forced her to go. She could have done the right thing and stayed home. Then we wouldn't be in this predicament."

"Okay, okay," Daniel tried to calm them down, "so I failed. I should have done something to convince her to stay home. Or, maybe I should have chosen Holly or Corey and let one of you deal with Joy, if you think you could have done better!"

"You think Corey has been easy?!" Gabriel threw back at him. "Chasing him through the woods trying to keep him from crashing into a tree? And trying to keep him from killing himself when he jumped off the cliff into the water?"

He paused in his tirade, looked at Robby and said, "I would have much rather had Holly."

Now it was Robby's turn to be surprised. "Like Holly is easy!" he snorted. "You weren't here yesterday when she tried to electrocute herself in the bathtub! Plus, she almost let Abigail back out of the yard in front of a truck. Oh no, Holly might be cute, but she certainly isn't an easy child to keep up with!"

"Okay, so they have all been challenging," Daniel summed it up. "I had to become a lug nut going seventy miles an hour down the highway to keep Joy's front wheel from falling off. This whole mission has been way more work than any of us had anticipated."

The three angels grew silent and hung their heads in defeat. They had managed to keep the Carter children safe so far, but not necessarily out of trouble. Did this mean they had failed their mission? Would they have a chance to redeem themselves? This was a new experience for all three of them, and none of them were quite sure where to go from here.

Gabriel shook his head slowly in resignation. "Yeah, they have all been hard to deal with. Maybe we just don't have what it takes to get this family back on course."

"I know I'm a little frazzled," Robby admitted. "No wonder Abigail asked for help. She's been dealing with this for a lot longer than we have."

The troubled trio all nodded their heads in agreement. Maybe they couldn't decide which child was the most challenging, but they could agree that Mom had been right in asking for help.

Finally Daniel spoke up. "You guys better get back to Holly and Corey," he suggested. "I'll hang out here and try to figure out what to do now."

He looked up at his partners, who nodded in agreement. They had been away for long enough, and should both get back to their respective subjects to make sure all was well. Plus, Joy was Daniel's responsibility, and he was a very capable individual. They felt confident that he would come up with a solution.

"Hey, man, we're here for you," Robby spoke up, before he flew away.

"That's right," Gabriel agreed. "We are a team, so let us know if there's anything we can do. And we'll let you know if we come up with any ideas, too."

Daniel waved his cohorts off and settled down under the apple tree. He would start by having a heart-to-heart conversation with Heaven in an effort to figure out how to help Joy and the Carter family. At first, he leaned against the tree and rested his head on the coarse surface of the tree trunk. As he did, he was overcome with the desire to give up and just return to his celestial home.

Maybe he shouldn't have come back to Earth. Maybe he

just wasn't ready to take on a mission. He had been so confident that he could handle whatever came his way. Yet, he had met his match with little, Harmonie "Joy" Carter. She had managed to continuously stay one step ahead of him, and he had needed to go above and beyond what he considered to be the call of duty to keep her safe. How had he known this would be so challenging? Maybe he should just call it quits.

And then what? he suddenly thought to himself. *What happens to Joy and her family if I give up?*

Daniel had never been a quitter, and wondered why he was ready to give up now. As bad as things seemed to be going, he knew quitting was not a solution. He had to see this mission through. To give up now could spell disaster for Joy. She might be at a turning point, if he could just find the right means of reaching her. He had seen the look of fear in her eyes when the police had shown up at the bar, and he knew she wasn't happy with the outcome. If he could just somehow reach her at this vulnerable point in time, it might change the course of her life.

He couldn't sit still any longer. There had to be something he could do. So, Daniel paced back and forth across the Carter front lawn, racking his brains and reaching out to the Highest Power to seek guidance. He thought back to his days on Earth, trying to recall tactics that had helped his clients succeed in taking control of their lives. He contemplated back to his trainings and college days, and cried out to God Himself to show him what to do.

Suddenly, Daniel's eyes lit up, as if all of Heaven had opened and given him the words he needed. It couldn't have been any clearer if the words had been scrolled across the sky. Six simple words that held so much truth.

The more he thought about it, the more convinced he became that these were the words Joy needed to hear. These were words that might make her connect her behavior with the consequences she had just experienced. Yet, even more, they were words that might help the whole family. He couldn't wait to share his insight with Gabe and Robby. He knew it would have to wait until morning, though, since the family was currently located in three separate lodgings. That would give him time to figure out how to present the phrase to the family. It had to be subtle enough so Joy wouldn't get defensive, as was her typical reaction. The challenge now would be waiting until morning. It just couldn't come soon enough, as far as he was concerned.

Joy Carter, have I got words of wisdom for you, Daniel thought triumphantly. *You almost won. I thought I had met my match with you, but you just wait until morning. Do I have something that you need to hear!*

With that, Daniel set about plotting his course of action.

<+><+><+>

CHAPTER 12
THE ULTIMATE FAMILY MEETING

The morning couldn't come quick enough for Daniel. If he had human feet, he would have worn out the grass in the front yard from pacing back and forth. He was relieved when he saw Russell hop into the family car shortly after sunrise to set off and retrieve his two absent children.

After returning home last night, Russell and Abigail had discussed how to handle Joy's predicament. They weren't sure if they should share the event with the other children, or keep them sheltered from what had happened. However, they had always wanted to be upfront and honest with their children. Plus, they hoped that the younger children would learn from the mistakes they witnessed in others. So on the ride home, Russell explained to Corey and Holly what had happened with Joy the night before.

Corey was stunned that his sister would have fallen into a situation like that. She had definitely been self-centered lately, but he didn't expect her to be lurking around bars and ending up at the police station.

"What was she thinking?" he asked his father in astonishment.

"I don't think she was thinking, son," Russell replied.

"I'll never do anything like that, Daddy," Holly reassured her father.

"I hope not, sweetie," Russell smiled back at her.

"So what are you going to give her for a punishment?" Corey questioned.

Russell just shrugged his shoulders. He had never had to deal with anything like this before. He had not been one to sneak into a bar as a kid, nor had any of his siblings. So, he wasn't sure how a parent should handle a problem like this.

"Maybe she needs a time-out," Holly suggested. She was still young enough so a time-out was an effective method of punishment.

"I wish it was that easy, sweetie," Russell said to his youngest child, "but Joy has kind of outgrown time-outs."

Russell let out an audible sigh and said, "Mom and I talked about it for a long time last night, but we haven't really come up with a solution yet."

Corey just nodded. Having lived with Joy for all of his fifteen years, and witnessed her recent behaviors, he could understand their dilemma.

Daniel breathed a sigh of relief when he saw the Carter family car pull back into the yard. Seeing Gabriel and Robert with the family, Daniel quickly called them over to share his exciting news with them.

"Hey, I think I heard from Heaven last night," he exclaimed. "Just one simple little phrase that has a lot of meaning to it, especially with all that we have been through with this family."

As Russell and the kids exited the car and headed inside, Daniel led his partners aside to share his revelation with them.

Russell and Abigail knew they probably needed a family meeting to discuss the situation, but they weren't quite sure how to approach it. It was something that affected them all, but Joy would certainly feel as though she were being singled out, with all fingers pointed directly at her. Instead of viewing this as a family matter with all members wanting to help, she would probably get defensive and take any advice as criticism.

The two parents had laid awake in bed for hours the night before, trying to determine what the next step should be. They had shared their feelings of inadequacy, yet they both knew they had done nothing wrong. They had each done all they could to make Joy happy in life, but apparently it hadn't been enough. Somehow, or somewhere, they must have failed in their parenting skills.

Abigail greeted Corey and Holly each with a hug when they came through the front door.

"Sorry about last night," she apologized. "I feel bad that we had to ditch you like that."

"It wasn't your fault," Corey reassured her, returning her hug, "and Ryan's family didn't mind anyway."

"I didn't mind, Mommy," Holly said cheerfully. "I like sleeping at Aunt Carrie's house, and she made me pancakes for breakfast!"

Abigail smiled and patted Holly on the head.

"Where's Joy?" Russell asked cautiously.

"She's still in her room," Abigail replied. "We haven't spoken yet. She hasn't come out, and I haven't dared to go in. I'm just afraid of what I might say to her."

Looking at the two children standing awkwardly in the kitchen, Mom said, "Why don't you two go watch TV for awhile until we figure out what we are doing today."

Corey and Holly were quick to comply. They anxiously headed off toward the living room, not sure they wanted to be in the middle of this family drama. Watching television sounded like a good alternative right about now.

Meanwhile, the trio of angels was having a discussion of their own out in the front yard. Daniel had shared with Gabriel and Robert how he had a revelation from Heaven, and that he thought this one, simple phrase could help to change the course of Joy's life.

"While everyone was sleeping last night," he explained, "I donned my human form and wrote this sign."

He showed them the sign, and then continued. "I think it will actually help all three of the kids. I just have to figure out what to do with it."

Both Gabriel and Robert read Daniel's sign and nodded. It was indeed simple, but was straight to the point.

"Well, why don't we all head inside and see what's going on," Gabriel suggested.

The angels joined the family inside the homestead, and saw that Joy was just rising. Corey and Holly were watching television in the living room, while Russell and Abigail were trying to relax over a cup of coffee at the kitchen table.

Coming out of her bedroom, Joy meekly said, "I think I'm going to go take a shower."

"That's fine, honey," Abigail said, trying to remain upbeat and positive.

"But then we need to discuss this," Russell spoke up, not wanting her to think they were going to let this go.

Joy humbly nodded her head, returned to her room to gather up her necessities, and headed into the bathroom.

Seeing an open opportunity, Daniel said, "I've got it! I'll just leave this note on Joy's bureau while she's in the bathroom. I just need a distraction so I can get in there."

Daniel had to say no more. Gabriel and Robby quickly hopped into motion. They flew into the living room and unbeknown to Corey and Holly, subtly took over the television screen. They hastily devised a hilarious commercial, which soon had both children laughing in hysterics. Abigail and Russell couldn't resist checking on them to see what was so funny. After the night they had just experienced, they could use a good laugh.

While the Carter family was being held captive by the antics of Gabe and Robby on the television, Daniel seized the opportunity to become human. Using his human hands and feet, he hurried into Joy's bedroom and strategically placed his handwritten sign in the middle of her bureau where she would be sure to see it upon her return. Exiting her room, he motioned to his television comedic partners that his mission was accomplished.

Gabe and Robby ended their "commercial" and smiled with glee as they watched the Carter family still reeling with laughter.

"I've never seen that commercial before," Corey laughed, still holding his side.

"It sure was funny," Holly agreed, still giggling herself.

Russell and Abigail shared a look of bliss while listening to their children laugh. This was the kind of family life they wanted — one with pure, honest, simple joy and happiness.

Smiling at the sounds of glee coming from the living room, Daniel asked, "So what was your commercial about? They really seemed to enjoy it."

"Oh, just something we came up with on the spur of the moment," Gabriel admitted.

"Yeah, just a little slapstick comedy," Robby agreed. "I did most of the slapstick, of course."

"Of course," Daniel agreed. "I would have expected that much. What was your product?"

"The funny thing is, we didn't really have one," Gabriel admitted.

Daniel chuckled, and then said, "Well, it looks like the

family enjoyed it so much, they didn't really even notice it wasn't advertising anything."

Hearing the laughter through the bathroom door, Joy had to know what was happening. Maybe she was missing something that she wanted to be a part of or maybe, for some reason, they were laughing at her. Either way, she felt the need to know what was going on.

Opening the door, she asked, "What's so funny?"

Everyone was startled by her entrance. They had been so caught up in the moment, they had forgotten all about Joy in the bathroom.

"We just saw the funniest commercial," Abigail explained.

"What was it about?" she asked.

The rest of the Carter family looked quizzically at each other, and then shrugged their shoulders.

"I don't really know," Corey explained, then starting to chuckle again he added, "but it sure was funny!"

Joy immediately resumed her defensive nature, assuming they just didn't want to tell her. "Whatever," she said, exiting back into the bathroom.

Russell and Abigail looked blankly at each other and shook their heads. Leave it to Joy to put a damper on any family jocularity. A moment later, Joy emerged from the bathroom carrying her belongings and headed toward her room as if on a mission. Abigail's heart sunk. She was acting as though she didn't want to be a part of this family anymore, like contact with them was a contagious disease.

In Joy's eyes, though, she was feeling humiliated. She felt as though everyone in her family was staring at her, wanting to confront her about what had happened last night. She didn't want to talk about it, or even admit that it had occurred. How could it have come to that? They were just going to listen to the music. How could they have ended up getting hauled off to the police station? Her parents weren't supposed to even know she had gone to the bar. Instead, they had needed to come to her rescue.

Russell and Abigail exchanged a frustrated look. They simply were not sure how to help Joy, or how they were going to even get through this day. It was rare that they were all together lately. Today, they were all in the same house, but at odds with the eldest child. Yet, before they had a chance to voice their thoughts, Joy let out with a wild cry from her bedroom.

"Okay, guys," Daniel said, giving his fellow angels a warning look, "anything can happen now. Be on your guard."

Both Gabriel and Robby nodded in agreement. They had no idea how Joy would handle Daniel's words of wisdom. She might embrace them and apply them to her life, but judging by her reaction so far, it sounded more like she would fly off the handle.

And that's just what she did. A moment later, she came flying out of her room with fire in her eyes.

"Alright, who's the wise guy that put this sign on my bureau?" she yelled at the innocent members of the Carter family sitting in the living room.

They looked from one to another, but none of them had a clue what she was talking about. So Abigail spoke up and asked, "What sign?"

"This one!" she demanded, waving the sign frantically in the air.

Abigail raised an eyebrow and turned to look at Russell. He was just as clueless, so he only shrugged his shoulders in reply.

"We don't know, Joy," he assured her. "We were all in the living room watching television while you were in the bathroom."

"Well, someone put it in there," she insisted. "It wasn't there when I left, and I don't think it's the least bit funny!"

Daniel looked anxiously at Gabe and Robby. He had been so sure this sign would help, but Joy seemed quite upset about it. Why did she always have to take things the wrong way? These were supposed to be words of encouragement, words of guidance, words that could help her make better decisions.

Curious about what it said, Russell asked, "Can I see it? Let's just take a look at it."

Joy walked over and handed it to her father, then dropped down on the couch beside her mother. She was still fuming, but after reading the sign, Russell donned a slight smile.

"Okay, so let's discuss this," he said, looking up brightly. "I don't think there is anything to be offended about here."

He held the sign up for the rest of the family to see and read, "It says, 'Poor choices carry high price tags.' So, let's think about that for a minute."

Starting with Joy, he looked at her and asked, "Can you think of any poor choices you have made recently, Joy?"

Joy hung her head in defeat and said, "I shouldn't have gone to the bar with Amber last night. I wasn't old enough to be there. I used a fake ID and had no right to be someplace where people were drinking and getting drunk."

Russell and Abigail exchanged a satisfied look. They were surprised that Joy had admitted to her actions. Maybe they were making progress here. They nodded slightly at each other, and traded a vague smile.

"Okay, true enough," Russell agreed. "So, what happened because of this poor choice?"

Without looking up, Joy softly replied, "I ended up at the police station, and you and Mom had to come rescue me."

Dad looked tenderly at his eldest child and asked, "And how did that make you feel?"

Joy didn't hesitate in her reply. "Terrible," she spoke up, "absolutely awful! I don't ever want to go through that again."

"Does that mean no more bars?" Dad asked gently.

Looking up at him sheepishly, Joy quietly said, "No more bars."

"So, I would think this sign applies here then," Russell said, looking at the sign in his hand again. "You made a poor choice last night, and it did carry a high price tag – humiliation, in your case."

Turning to look at Corey, he continued with his momentum. "Okay, Corey," he said, addressing his son, "can you think of a poor choice you might have made?"

"Driving my ATV into Mom's new car?" Corey suggested.

"Oh, yeah," Russell agreed with is son, "that was definitely a poor choice with a very high price tag. It cost a lot of money to get that fixed."

Turning to face his son, he asked, "And how did you feel when it happened?"

Glancing over at Joy, Corey said, "Just like Joy, I felt awful. I know Mom has always wanted a new car, and I put a huge dent in it. It made me feel very irresponsible."

Russell nodded, feeling excited that his kids really seemed to be getting it. "So, what could you have done differently?"

Corey hung his head and thought a minute. Then looking up he said, "I should have been more careful. I shouldn't have been driving my ATV so fast in the front yard. If I had been paying attention, Mom's car wouldn't have been damaged as bad as it was. I need to slow down and be more aware of my surroundings."

Russell and Abigail couldn't believe how well this family meeting seemed to be going. For once, everyone was actively involved and connecting their behavior with the consequence. Two out of the three children had definitely scored well in their replies, but what about the youngest one?

Russell turned to face Holly, not sure that she was getting the gist of the meeting. She was one who truly had trouble with the behavior and consequence connection. However, Holly was prepared and ready for his approach.

"Holly?" Dad asked, looking questioningly at her. "Can you think of a poor choice you made that had a high price tag?"

"Yup," she promptly replied, "when I stood up in the apple tree and fell out."

Russell was clearly surprised with her quick answer. He hadn't expected her to be so in tune with the conversation, let alone come up with a behavior that had been costly.

Nodding his head in agreement with her, he said, "That's true, it was a poor choice. And how did it affect you?"

"It hurt a lot," she said, pursing her lips and bobbing her head up and down. "And I got tired of wearing the cast," she added.

"So, how could you keep it from happening again?" Abigail asked her daughter.

"Don't climb the tree anymore," Holly smiled jubilantly.

The Carter parents were stunned at the response of their children. They couldn't have been more proud or delighted with their answers, plus they felt simply ecstatic with the involvement of their children. Why couldn't every family meeting be this successful? This was the whole point of having them, to try to figure out what the problem was, and then resolve it as a team. Each child had effectively identified a problem, and had taken it a step further to come up with a solution.

Russell looked from his eldest child down through to the youngest and smiled fondly at each of them.

"So, are we all in agreement that this sign makes perfect sense?" he asked.

All three heads nodded in agreement. Daniel, Gabriel, and Robert started giving each other high fives. At first they had feared the sign was going to cause a battle, but Daniel had been right. These were words that could help redirect the Carter children, if they were willing to remember them and abide by them.

"Okay," said Russell with satisfaction. "I think maybe we should frame this sign and hang it someplace visible where we will all see it and remember to follow its advice."

He paused a moment, and then added, "And since the day is still young and it is beautiful weather outside, what do you say we all hop in the car and take a drive to the beach?"

"Can we stop and get ice cream on the way home?" Holly asked.

"You bet!" Russell replied.

"You guys did such a good job with family meeting," Abigail spoke up, "that you all deserve both a day at the beach and ice cream, too."

"So, go gather your things and let's get headed!" Dad instructed his family.

The Carter kids were quick to comply, jumping up and heading off to gather their belongings for the beach. The two parents just watched in amazement for a moment, still not sure that what they had just witnessed had really happened.

Abigail stood up and gave Russell a big hug.

"That was the best family meeting ever," she said with a smile.

"Nothing short of amazing," he agreed with her.

"Do you think they finally understand the purpose of family meetings?" Abigail questioned her husband.

He paused to contemplate her question for a moment, then smiled down at her and said, "Naw, I think it was an anomaly. But it was definitely a nice change!"

She gave him a playful slap on the arm and said, "You can call it an anomaly if you want, but I call it progress."

Deciding they needed to gather up a few things of their own before heading to the beach, Russell and Abigail exited the living room. Daniel, Gabriel, and Robby were just as ecstatic about the way the meeting had gone as were the Carter parents. In fact, they might have been even more excited. They felt they had finally made a difference in this family and gotten through to the children. They were so ecstatic that they started ringing their silver bells.

Abigail paused for a moment, remembering a day a few months ago when she had sat in a lonely, vacant church pew seeking a sign from God. Had she heard bells that day as a sign? Had she just heard bells today?

Turning to face her husband, she asked, "Did you just hear bells?"

"What?" he asked, absentmindedly, while taking off his shoes to put his sandals on.

She halted and listened intently, but then decided it was nothing. "Never mind," she said, continuing on her quest to get ready for the beach. "I guess I'm just hearing things."

<+><+><+>

CHAPTER 13
ANGELS UNAWARE

Daniel, Gabriel, and Robert stayed with the Carter family until each of the three children had reached adulthood. There were many times when they wondered if they would accomplish their mission of keeping the children safe throughout their childhood and guiding them into the realm of adulthood. It became especially challenging when Holly started driving. Gabe may have been concerned with Corey's driving skills, but Robby definitely had his work cut out for him with Holly. However, all three children finally managed to graduate from high school, with no more broken bones or major accidents, and went on to establish thriving careers.

Joy's experience at the bar proved to be instrumental indeed, and the incident stayed with her for the rest of her life. It not only put a fear in her heart of developing a faulty record, but also opened her eyes to the realization that it was not the lifestyle she wanted for herself. Plus, it was not a heritage she would have wanted to pass on to her children. It was the one and only encounter she ever wanted to have with law enforcement, with her being on the wrong side of the law, anyway. She suddenly found purpose for her life, and knew what she wanted to do. Drinking, smoking, and hanging out in bars were not a part of that plan. She determined to set her course, and then worked fervently to achieve her goal.

So, following her graduation from high school, she went on to college and acquired a degree in child psychology. Her focus was geared toward helping children find their place in life, so they wouldn't seek the misguided perceptions that come with the use of alcohol or drugs. By helping them to believe in themselves and be satisfied with the simple pleasures in life, she hoped she would be able to help them avoid developing habits that would only hold them back, or reek havoc with their lives. Avoidance of substance abuse became her primary focus.

Since Joy was so much closer to adulthood than were her siblings, Daniel's mission ended sooner than his cohorts. However, he popped in on her periodically at college just to make sure all was well, and to provide a little extra guidance when she needed it. His visits also gave him the opportunity to check in with Gabriel and Robby, and offer them his support and words of encouragement.

Knowing Corey, it shouldn't come as a surprise to learn that he started a small engine repair shop. For him, it was more than just a dream come true. Now he could not only continue to work (or play) with all terrain vehicles, but he would also get paid for it. His love for fast, small motored vehicles never waned. He just couldn't get enough of riding ATVs, and couldn't believe his good fortune of developing a career in working with them. He would never need to outgrow his passion for ATVs. As an adult, not only could he continue to ride them, but he could earn an income to support a family while he did it. Life couldn't get any better than that!

And as for Holly, she grew up to be a baker. Baking was her passion and she dwelt in a state of blissfulness while making cupcakes, cookies, or just about anything that was sweet and edible. She started out working as an apprentice in a bakery, but then moved on to establish a store of her own. One would not be surprised to find that she named it Holly's Heavenly Delights. Through years of experience, she learned to actually make delicious chocolate cupcakes, which was a little ironic in itself. She often thought back to the night of the family cookout when her mother had told everyone about her "chocolate bottomed" cupcakes. Now, instead of having to cut the burnt bottoms off, everyone raved about how delicious her chocolate cupcakes were. No one in town made a more delectable cupcake than the little "cupcake" herself.

Russell and Abigail couldn't have been prouder of their three children. They were relieved to watch them not only reach adulthood and graduate from high school, but were also pleased with their career choices. They found that perseverance and determination in raising their children properly had paid off. Plus, the unknown help from three heavenly visitors was beneficial as well, whether they were aware of it or not.

Daniel, Gabriel, and Robert were eventually reunited as a trio again in Heaven, each having accomplished their mission of assisting their Carter child into the status of adulthood. Robby, of course, was the last angel to return home. He had missed the companionship of Daniel and Gabriel in the final years of Holly's childhood and was extremely happy for the reunification with his friends. They had a good time sharing stories about the events with the Carter children. Having been apart for awhile, there was a lot to talk about once they were back together.

Their mission was celebrated as a success in Heaven, and God Himself congratulated them for a job well done. The three angels were extremely thankful that the brawl at the bar never came up as a topic in the divine vastness of Heaven. The heavenly beings were probably all aware of it, but they either chose to avoid the topic or didn't dare to bring up. Being a delicate subject, not one of the three angels was eager to discuss it either.

Daniel, Gabriel, and Robby had all feared losing their wings that night. The event had definitely not gone according to their liking, but it had seemed to serve as a pivotal turning point for Joy. From that night on, her life seemed to take on new meaning. She was driven after that, having found her purpose in life and her determination to achieve it was amazing. That alone may have been the reason the heavenly beings didn't raze the subject. It had brought about a positive outcome, not just for Joy, but for the whole Carter family.

The sign Daniel had made for the family stating "Poor choices carry high price tags" is still framed and posted in the Carter family kitchen. It proved to be a useful tool throughout the rest of the children's adolescent years. Any time one of them appeared to be making a poor choice, either Abigail or Russell would point out the sign and encourage them to think about what they were doing. It truly was a message from Heaven, designed as a guiding light to help them through their darkest hours.

As for the future happenings for Daniel, Gabriel, and Robert, well don't think that they gave up after their first mission. Having helped the Carter family succeed had such an impact on all three of them that they were quick to volunteer and come to the aid of other families in need. They have since taken on several missions, returning frequently to Earth, and sharing their expertise with other families as well.

Not all the assignments they take on require that they remain invisible and unknown. In some circumstances, as was the case with Joy, they have needed to take on human form to aid their subject.

If you look carefully, there are times when you might still see them. One never knows where they might turn up next. They are likely to be anywhere, at any time, helping anyone. They might show up as a police officer, firefighter, teacher, janitor, highway worker, street sweeper, Sunday school teacher, store clerk, taxi cab driver, gas station attendant, the elderly man sitting on the park bench…… Is it really just a chance encounter, or is it a heavenly being sent to help you?

"…for some have entertained angels unawares."
Hebrews 13:2

<+><+><+>

EPILOGUE
WISDOM FROM THE PEARLY GATES

The angels stood before the austere, pearly gates of Heaven. Daniel, Gabriel, and Robert were finally together again, having completed their mission with the Carter family, and were about to return as a trio to their heavenly home. No matter how many times they had seen the pearly gates, they never ceased to be amazed at their awesomeness. There was nothing on Earth that could compare to the beauty of what stood before them.

"Well, men, we did it," Daniel said, turning to congratulate his cohorts.

"Yes, we did," Gabriel agreed, "although I must admit there were times when I questioned whether we would be successful or not."

"Huh!" scoffed Robby. "The thought of failure never crossed my mind!"

Daniel and Gabriel turned to face their partner. They tipped their heads and raised an eyebrow, both thinking of many times when he thought he was going to fail. Neither of them said a word, but Robby got the message.

"Okay, okay," he agreed, "there were a few times when it did occur to me that we might not be successful."

The other two angels smiled and nodded their heads. It had been their first mission, and a learning experience for all three of them. Next time, they would be more prepared and gather as much information about those they are going to help before jumping into the situation.

Turning to face the gates of glory, Gabriel asked, "Are we ready men?"

Daniel paused a moment, and then said, "I feel like I should share some words of wisdom before walking through the gates."

Gabriel and Robert thought about it, and then nodded their heads in agreement.

"Okay, that sounds like it makes sense," Gabriel said. Turning to look at Robby, he asked, "Are you in a hurry to return?"

Robby shook his head and said, "Hey, I've got all the time in the world." Then thinking about what a funny statement that was coming from an angel, he added, "I mean, I've got eternity ahead of me!"

Daniel smiled and said, "Well, let's share some insight as to what we learned from this experience."

He stepped back and stood straight and tall, taking on a rigid pose, almost as if addressing a large auditorium of listeners.

WORDS OF WISDOM FROM DANIEL

"If there is one thing I learned from this mission on Earth, it was to find satisfaction in the simple pleasures of life. A family cookout, a day at the beach, or even gatherings with relatives can be very rewarding. There is nothing simple about substance abuse, whether it is alcohol, drugs, or cigarettes. They each can carry a high price tag - such as alcoholism, drug addiction, or cancer.

"Never underestimate the power of alcohol and drugs. Don't allow yourself to have grandiose thoughts by thinking that you can play games with substance abuse and come out the winner."

Daniel paused, looked at his buddies and said, "Did you know that some people believe things like this can happen to others, but never to them? But the fact of the matter is - it's just not true. Substance abuse is a powerful force that can swallow up the strongest of individuals. It isn't just a desire or thought process that can be controlled at will. It can become a physical craving that demands attention and execution. And it doesn't care who it kills or what life it disrupts. Plus, substance abuse affects more than an individual. It becomes a family problem, and sometimes affects a whole community.

"Joy found that she had a lot to offer others in life. However, if she hadn't heeded the advice from Heaven, she could have ruined her life with an addiction. What she didn't realize was that a habit which begins as a willing act can take control of your life. And it could take only one wild party to destroy your future. So, don't compromise the quality of your life by starting a bad habit that will rule your future. When your friends want you to go out partying, remind yourself that you only have one body. Don't abuse it or cause damage to it. Treat it with respect. What you do in your younger years can affect the quality of your life forever.

"Instead of following your friends into a compromising situation, in its place suggest an expedition to the mall, a night at the movies, or a trip to the beach. There are lots of ways to enjoy life that do not involve the danger of substance abuse. And if they still want to party, find someone else to hang out with. You don't need to follow their example or allow them talk you into ruining your body as well."

Turning to see his angelic partners with folded arms and silently watching him, Daniel straightened his back, pulled his shoulders back, and said, "And so, in conclusion, I would remind everyone that they only have one body, so honor it and treat it with respect."

Gabriel and Robert applauded their fellow angel, and Daniel took a mock bow.

"That was very good," Robby complimented him.

"Yes, and we could really hear the drug and alcohol counselor side of you in that speech," Gabriel smiled at him.

"That's true," Daniel commented, "it wasn't anything I am not already knowledgeable about. Through my career on Earth, I met with many people who had thrown away years of their lives," he paused to look at Gabriel and Robby before adding, "some times even decades, to substance abuse. I saw how many times it tore whole families apart. And at times, I read articles in the newspaper about a community turned upside down by an act that someone dealing with substance abuse committed."

He paused for a moment, then looking at Gabriel and Robert added, "Unfortunately, sometimes they were my clients."

The angels shook their heads sadly, knowing how poorly it must have made Daniel feel. No wonder he was so devoted to keeping Joy on the right track. Then, not wanting to linger on negative thoughts, Daniel quickly returned to his speech.

"So, I am very pleased that Joy made the right choice and decided to live a clean life. Plus, her experience was a good learning tool for her younger siblings."

Daniel hesitated, and then added, "You know, I felt like such a failure the night Joy got arrested, but I wonder if the Father allowed that to happen. It proved to be a real wake up call for Joy."

"Hmm," Gabe pondered, "you might be right about that. Some people believe that everything happens for a reason."

"So maybe He did allow it to happen," Robby commented, "but you can be sure I'm not going to ask!"

Having finished with his words of wisdom, Daniel asked, "Does anyone else have something they want to share?"

Gabe looked thoughtful for a minute, but Robby just shrugged his shoulders and waved Daniel off.

"I could probably share some thoughts, too," Gabe spoke up.

"Then you go for it, my man," Robby smiled.

WORDS OF WISDOM FROM GABRIEL

Clearing his throat and addressing his small audience, Gabriel spoke up.

"There were times when it was very challenging for me to keep Corey safe. A few times, if I hadn't been there to help him, I'm not sure how he would have faired. It's one thing to have fun, but it's another thing to be reckless and foolish.

"When Corey jumped off the cliff to dive into the water below, that was definitely a time when I wasn't sure I could keep him safe. You can imagine how relieved I was to see him emerge from the water and walk out safely onto the shore."

Turning to look at his angelic friends, he asked, "What was he thinking?"

The other two angels simply shrugged their shoulders and gave Gabe a baffled look.

Returning to his speech, he continued, "Corey went on to experience the pleasure of graduating from high school and establishing his dream career. If one of his reckless adventures had gone awry, he might have missed that opportunity."

He paused for a thoughtful moment, and then added, "And watching those girls when he was supposed to be driving? He could have crashed into that truck. If I hadn't been there, it might not have had a good outcome."

Gabriel stopped and hung his head. Looking up at Dan and Robby, he admitted, "Of course, I was watching the girls, too."

He quickly looked over his shoulder to see if any other angelic beings were close enough to hear his admission of imperfect behavior. He was relieved to see they were the only angels present.

Robby chuckled and said, "It's a good thing I wasn't there. He probably would have hit the truck, because I would have been totally distracted by the girls."

Gabe smiled at him and nodded his head. "That thought had occurred to me," he mumbled quietly. Then seeing Robby giving him a curious look, he quickly continued.

"So, what I'm trying to say is this: Don't take risks that could cause you to miss out on the finer qualities of life. You are just as human as the next guy, and accidents can happen to anyone. Do your best to protect yourself, and don't be foolish. Be aware of your surroundings and take every necessary precaution to keep yourself safe. You only have one life to live, so live it wisely."

Robby started to clap, but Gabriel quickly interrupted him.

"Wait a minute," he said, "I'm not quite done yet."

Robby formed a silent "Oh," and Gabriel smiled in return. Straightening his shoulders, he said, "So, here's my conclusion. Like Daniel said with his substance abuse concern, don't take chances. Your body may not be able to recover from the damage you have caused. Unnecessary risks could leave you maimed or crippled."

He paused for a moment, at which time Robby added, "Or dead – like me."

Gabriel had momentarily forgotten that Robby had died from taking a foolish, unnecessary risk of his own.

"Oh, Robby, I wasn't directing that toward you," he apologized.

"That's okay," Robby spoke up. "You're absolutely correct. I never got the chance to finish my lifetime on Earth due to my reckless behavior. That's why I was so anxious to take on this mission. I wanted to go back and see what I was missing, so no need to apologize."

The three angels stood awkwardly for a short space of time, and then Daniel asked, "So, are you ready to wrap it up, Gabriel? Have you summed up your conclusion?"

"Oh, my conclusion," Gabe said softly. He pondered it briefly, and then resumed his formal stance.

"Okay, here it is," he began. "Life is meant to be fun, but don't forget to be safe. Wear you helmet, watch your speed, and don't be so reckless that you lose control. Pain is not gain. Don't think that accidents can happen to others but not you. You are not invincible. So be careful, think things through, and let safety be your goal."

"That was great!" Daniel complimented him.

Then the two senior angels turned to face Robby.

"Okay, Robert," Daniel addressed him, "What do you have to say?"

Robby was clearly surprised. He threw his hands into the air and took a step backwards.

"Really?" he questioned, with a look of disbelief on his face. "You expect words of wisdom from me? I'm just a fun-loving guy who left life way too early from doing something stupid. What advice do I have to offer?"

"Don't be so hard on yourself," Daniel told him. "You've been through a lot since then, so I'm sure you have something to say."

"Sure you do," Gabriel agreed. "Give it a try."

"Okay, okay, here goes," Robby started. He rubbed his chin and stared at his feet before finding the right words to begin with.

"Alright, I think I've got something," he finally spoke up.

WORDS OF WISDOM FROM ROBERT

"Heaven is a wonderful place, but there are a lot of things we don't have up here," he paused and looked at his angelic friends, as if to see if they were in agreement. Not sure where he was heading with his speech, they both gave brief nods encouraging him to continue.

"I mean things like warm hugs from the people we love back on Earth. And do you know what else we don't have?"

He paused and looked at Daniel and Gabriel for an answer. When they just shrugged their shoulders, he jubilantly cried out, "Pancakes! We don't have pancakes here. I would have given anything to take a bite of those scrumptious looking pancakes Abigail made for her family. Yum!"

He took a break from his speech long enough to close his eyes and rub his stomach. Then suddenly his eyes flew open and he added, "Oh, and barbeques, too! We don't have barbeques in Heaven. Man, those burgers looked delicious!"

He licked his lips, and the other two angels couldn't help but laugh.

"You know, of all three kids, Holly chose the best profession," Robby stated. Continuing his thought, he added, "She chose food! She's the man!"

"She's a girl, Robby," Gabriel stated the obvious.

"Huh?" Robby started, and then quickly added, "Oh, I know that. It's just a saying."

Daniel and Gabriel chuckled again, and then Daniel tried to round Robby up and get him back on track.

"So, we know you miss the food," he observed, "but what are your words of wisdom?"

Robby stared off into space with a thoughtful look on his angelic face, and finally spoke up.

"I don't really have any words of wisdom, so I'll borrow yours," he said, facing Daniel. "Poor choices carry high price tags. I think that phrase makes a whole lot of sense. Every action or behavior is going to produce a consequence, so think before you act. That way, you can avoid an outcome or an ending that you may not want."

"That's good," Gabriel encouraged him.

"Anything else?" Daniel pressured him, "or are we ready to make our way through the pearly gates and go home?"

"Well, hold on just a minute," Robby said slowly. "I think I have a little more to offer."

Mimicking his partners, he stood straight, cleared his throat, and began his concluding comments to his audience of two. In a strong, authoritative voice, he spoke out.

"My brothers and sisters in the Lord," he bellowed out, "Live life to its fullest. Embrace each day as though it were your last. Love those around you. Be thankful for the food on your table. Enjoy the smell of burgers cooking on the grill, the feel of the sunshine on your back, the taste of pancakes with pure maple syrup," he paused and smiled at Daniel and Gabriel before continuing, "and let the sound of laughter be music to your ears. Treat life as a gift, and try to enjoy every minute of it."

When he had finished his speech, he turned to look at his two close buddies.

"How did I do, guys?" he asked them. "Was that okay?"

"I am truly impressed, Robert," Daniel complimented him. "That was not bad at all. I'm very proud of you."

"Maybe some of those Sunday morning church services with Holly and Abigail sunk in a little," Gabriel joked with him.

The trio turned to face the massive pearly gates, which slowly began to swing open to allow them entrance into their heavenly home. Both Daniel and Gabriel reached over to pat their buddy in the middle on the back as they began their passage back into glory.

"You are full of surprises," Daniel said to Robert.

"Yeah, I didn't know you had it in you," Gabriel agreed.

"You have definitely come a long way," Dan added.

"See, I wasn't sleeping during those church services," Robby joked. "I was paying attention."

"There might be hope for you yet," Gabe joked, as they strolled jovially through the gates.

Both Daniel and Gabriel turned to face their fellow angel, who only grinned in return and replied, "I sure hope so!"

<+><+><+>

ACKNOWLEDGEMENTS

The amazing thing about God is that while we are trying to figure out what we want to do when we grow up, He is paving the way for us to do it. When we finally arrive at our destiny, we can look back and see how methodically everything was orchestrated along the way.

Did my sister, Debbe Femiak, know she would someday be the artist who illustrates my books? When my sister, Linda Wright, took her first job as a typesetter and moved into the field of proofreading, did she know that one day she would be the family proofreader? And my niece, Michelle Wright, chose the field of graphic arts, which falls nicely into place with the book publishing needs.

While sometimes life can feel like a jigsaw puzzle with a few pieces out of place, we need to remember that God holds all the pieces in His hands. And in His time, He is putting them all into the proper place, right where they all belong. Then finally, as if observing from foreign eyes, we realize we have a completed work of art that's worth sharing.

I must primarily give God the glory for the completion of this book. It was years in the making, and while the characters in this story were products of my imagination, this book could never have reached completion without the final touches of my talented family. So thanks to everyone involved for your help in giving life to the Carter family and *Angels for Abigail*. I couldn't have done it without you.

OTHER BOOKS BY THE AUTHOR

Everybody has a bad day sometimes, but Mary Davis is having twelve of them – in a row! With a husband named Joseph, this couple knew Christmas would always be special to them. But packing twelve adult children and their families into one day of holiday fun proves to be less than joyful.

So Mary has come up with the perfect plan. She will invite each child to come home, one day at a time, thus stretching out the holiday season and avoiding the chaos of a houseful of not-so-holiday cheer. With a plan like that, what could possibly go wrong?

But day after day of her holiday plan leaves Mary scrambling to try to save the day. With a resilient attitude (and the support of her faithful husband) she somehow manages to survive all twelve days.

A Twelve Davis Christmas *is a comical view of a mother's love for her children, her efforts to give them her best, with a blend of Murphy's Law folded in. If anything can go wrong, it will happen to Mary and Joseph Davis – and their tribe of twelve.*

Kitty Litter: Thoughts from the Heart *is a sprinkling of uplifting thoughts, designed to give life a fresh, new aroma and help the reader see past the unpleasant aspects of life. It is comprised of three sections:*

- *The Art of Living*
- *The Joys of Parenting*
- *For the Spirit.*

Some thoughts are geared toward encouraging overwhelmed parents. Others are basic thoughts on the components of life itself and things that cross our paths simply as a side effect of being human. Some articles take on a spiritual tone and address the deeper meanings in life.

Wherever you may be on your walk in life, ***Kitty Litter: Thoughts from the Heart*** *has a message for you. Don't give up on this thing called life. It has too much to offer to waste time hanging out in the litter box.*

Let ***Kitty Litter*** *help you muster up some courage, put a smile back on your face, and find the strength to step out of the litter box to give life another chance.*

Jacob Miller was a good kid. He had been born into a respectable family, with loving parents who instilled positive morals and values in him. From the beginning of his life, they had worked hard at teaching him right from wrong. Yet, his childhood hadn't been perfect. Several traumas happened in the early stages of Jacob's childhood that had left him questioning the meaning of life. He had faced sleepless nights and days of heartache as he tried to make sense of it all.

However, Jacob Miller was a resilient child. He had always had a happy-go-lucky attitude, and he knew that he could rise above it all. Life had to have meaning and purpose, and he would figure out where he fit into all of it. As he grew older and became an adult, he determined the hardships of life would not hold him down or lead him astray. He would take charge and find true intention for his life. But, did he control his life, or did life control him?

Thirty Seconds to Life is a story that shows how life can sometimes fall apart, even for those who have had a good upbringing and the best of intentions. While the characters are fictional, the story is based on actual events. What would become of Jacob Miller? Would he ever get his life back again, or was a life behind bars all he would ever know? How had such a good, compassionate kid come to an act like this? What had gone so wrong in his life to have robbed him of his morals and allowed him to make such a dreadful choice?

CHILDREN'S BOOKS BY THE AUTHOR

After the Snowflakes is a fully illustrated children's book about winter time activities. Each beautifully illustrated page shows a different event that celebrates fun things we can do after the snowflakes fall, including a few pages showing how different snowflakes could look. It ends with a playful poem about the uniqueness of snowflakes, encouraging the reader to get outside and enjoy the winter.

✭✭✭✭✭✭✭

Sunny Boy is an illustrated children's book that discusses the role of the sun from an animated perpective. He starts to feel rejected when people don't appreciate him, but comes to realize the importance of the role he plays in the world around him. It is also a story of relationships and working together, as he forms a true friendship with Whispi the Cloud.

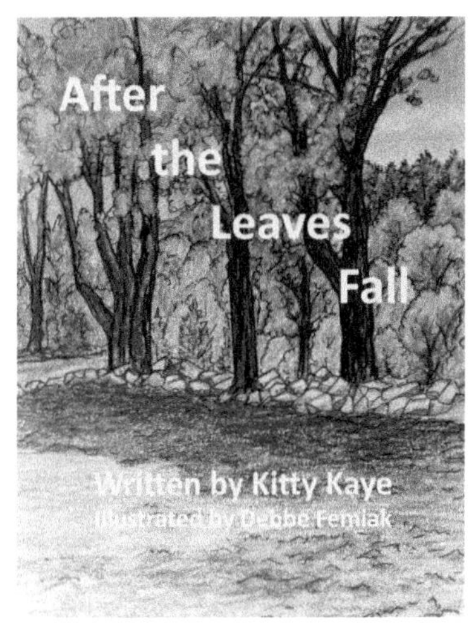

After the Leaves Fall is a beautifully illustrated children's book about the season of autumn. Each illustrated pages shows various activites to participate in after the leaves have fallen. Also included are pages showing the different shapes and colors of leaves. It winds down with a poem about autumn leaves, which encourages the reader to enjoy the colorful season of fall.

☆ ☆ ☆ ☆ ☆ ☆ ☆

Grandma Kitty's Coloring Book of Poetry is a book for coloring, filled with encouraging poetry verses. The children's verses are to help build self-esteem and promote acceptable behaviors. The adult verses are for those who have faced challenging situations. Each page has an illustration to color and is suitable for framing upon completion.

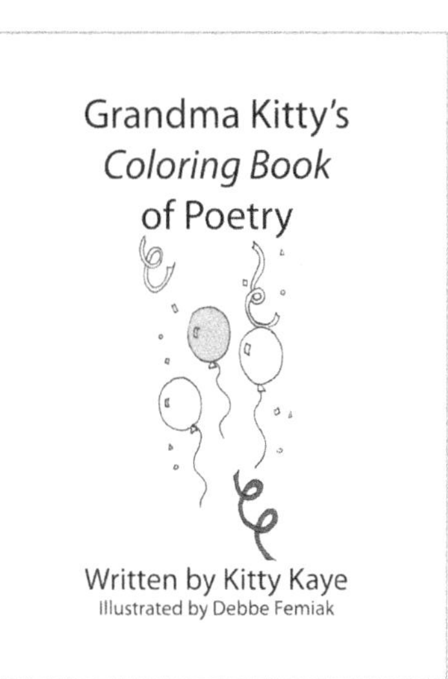

www.ingramcontent.com/pod-product-compliance
Lightning Source LLC
Chambersburg PA
CBHW070359200726
48294CB00003B/989